"Is what happened between us last night upsetting you?"

"Yes." Her voice wasn't much more than a whisper.

"Why?"

"Because we have a professional relationship. It shouldn't have happened. I shouldn't have allowed myself to—"

"Get so out of control?" Jack finished for her. "I was, too. Neither of us could have stopped. I wanted you." He gazed lingeringly at her lovely face. "I still want you. I think I have from the moment you walked into my office. You make me feel…" Jack shook his head. "That's it. You make me feel. I look at you—touch you—and I discover emotions I didn't know I was capable of."

"It wasn't supposed to happen like this."

Jack pulled her into his arms and held her close. "Last night was as natural for both of us as breathing. It was inevitable."

Dear Reader,

Everyone loves Linda Turner, and it's easy to see why, when she writes books like this month's lead title. *The Proposal* is the latest in her fabulous miniseries, THE LONE STAR SOCIAL CLUB. Things take a turn for the sexy when a straitlaced lady judge finds herself on the receiving end of an irresistible lawyer's charms as he tries to argue her into his bed. The verdict? Guilty—of love in the first degree.

We've got another miniseries, too: Carla Cassidy's duet called SISTERS. You'll enjoy *Reluctant Wife,* and you'll be eagerly awaiting its sequel, *Reluctant Dad,* coming next month. Reader favorite Marilyn Pappano is back with *The Overnight Alibi,* a suspenseful tale of a man framed for murder. Only one person can save him: the flame-haired beauty who spent the night in question in his bed. But where is she? And once he finds her, what is she hiding? Brittany Young joins us after writing twenty-six books for Silhouette Romance and Special Edition. *The Ice Man,* her debut for the line, will leave you eager for her next appearance. Nancy Gideon is back with *Let Me Call You Sweetheart,* a tale of small-town scandals and hot-running passion. And finally, welcome first-time author Monica McLean. *Cinderella Bride* is a fabulous marriage-of-convenience story, a wonderful showcase for this fine new author's talents.

And after you read all six books, be sure to come back next month, because it's celebration time! Intimate Moments will bring you three months' worth of extra-special books with an extra-special look in honor of our fifteenth anniversary. Don't miss the excitement.

Leslie J. Wainger
Senior Editor and Editorial Coordinator

Please address questions and book requests to:
Silhouette Reader Service
U.S.: 3010 Walden Ave., P.O. Box 1325, Buffalo, NY 14269
Canadian: P.O. Box 609, Fort Erie, Ont. L2A 5X3

THE ICE MAN

BRITTANY YOUNG

Published by Silhouette Books

America's Publisher of Contemporary Romance

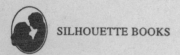 SILHOUETTE BOOKS

ISBN 0-373-07849-8

THE ICE MAN

Books by Brittany Young

BRITTANY YOUNG

lives and writes in Racine, Wisconsin. She has traveled to most of the countries that serve as the settings for her books and finds the research into the language, customs, history and literature of these countries among the most demanding and rewarding aspects of her writing.

Thanks to Cathy Perez, for her perfect Spanish
Thanks to *Inkapirka*, for their glorious music

Prologue

It was two o'clock in the morning. Jack Allessandro stood in his semidarkened office, and as the ferocious music of Béla Bartók filled it from corner to corner, he looked down at the nearly deserted Chicago street twenty stories below. He raised the half-full glass of scotch to his lips and took a drink.

He looked like what he was—a very successful businessman—from the conservative cut of his dark hair to the fit of his expensive suit. His jacket was neatly laid over the arm of the leather couch. His tie was loosened and the sleeves of his pristine white shirt were rolled halfway up his forearms. He was a powerful-looking man—tall, dark complected and broad shouldered. Women had thrown themselves at him since he was a teenager, and he had taken some of them up on what they'd offered.

But his heart had remained untouched.

Maybe that was just the way it would always be for him. Maybe he was incapable of loving a woman any way but physically.

Jack took another drink.

Lately he'd found himself thinking about having children. The older he grew, the more he thought about it. Of course, thinking about it and doing something about it were two different things.

Jack didn't know what he'd expected. Perhaps that he'd look at a woman one day—one particular woman—and realize that she and only she was the one he wanted as the mother of his child.

Well, he'd looked at a lot of women over the years and never once had that thought crossed his mind.

And as common as it was these days, he didn't want a child without a wife.

Perhaps he should just settle on someone, bite the bullet and get married. The woman he was currently seeing had some good qualities. He wasn't in love with her, but he was fond of her. That could grow into something deeper over time. She had certainly made her feelings for him obvious.

"I knew I'd find you still in your office."

Jack turned to find his younger sister standing in the doorway. "Patty," he said with a rare smile as he put down his drink and crossed the office to embrace her. "What are you doing here at this hour? You should be at home with your husband and daughter."

"I've been on duty at the hospital for the past thirty-six hours. I'm at the point where I'm too tired to drive myself home. Is it okay if I bunk with you tonight?"

"Of course."

Patty pointed at her brother's drink. "Do you have one of those for me?"

Jack went to the bar and mixed another scotch while Patty turned down the Bartók, sank into a chair across from Jack's desk and propped up her aching feet.

"Thanks," said Patty when her brother handed her the drink. "So why aren't you ever at your apartment? All you have to do is get on the elevator and go straight up. It's your building, after all."

"Long workdays."

Patty quirked an eyebrow. "Is that the only reason?"

"There's nothing really to go home to," said Jack quietly as he sat down. "I sleep there. That's pretty much it."

"And whose fault is that?"

"I know, I know."

"You work too much. You always have."

"Perhaps. But it's a choice I've made."

Patty gazed with warm brown eyes at the big brother she loved with all her heart. "No, you didn't, Jack. It was thrust upon you the day you took me out of our grandparents' home to raise me yourself. If it weren't for you, I would never have made it through medical school," she said softly. "I probably wouldn't have made it through high school." She looked at Jack for a long, quiet moment. "I think about that a lot, Jack. You're the one who made the life I live now possible. You were so focused on raising me and building this company that you didn't have time left for yourself. But now you do. Now you can afford to sit back, relax and enjoy your life."

"Who says I'm not enjoying it?"

"I do."

"Patty..."

"I can't even remember the last time I heard you laugh out loud. And the only time you smile is around my daughter or me."

"I've never been much of a smiler."

"You would be if you had someone to share your life with."

A corner of Jack's mouth curved upward. "It's just like a happily married woman to assume that's the answer for everyone else."

"It is."

"I have yet to meet a woman I would want to be married to."

"Have you really looked?"

"Odd that this should come up. I was just thinking about it."

"And did you arrive at any conclusions?"

"No conclusions. Just questions."

"Such as?"

"Maybe I'm asking for too much. Maybe the kind of woman I think I can love doesn't exist."

"She exists, all right. You just haven't met her yet."

"So you believe in soul mates?"

"I can't say that I did until I met my Kevin, but I do now. Somewhere out there, Jack, is the one woman in the world who is your other half. I know it."

"For such an educated woman, you talk a lot of nonsense." His words were blunt but his tone was gentle.

"You call it nonsense now, but I'm going to remind you of this conversation when you finally do meet Her.''

Jack took another swallow of his drink. ''I don't know. I was thinking that maybe I should just marry Barbara.''

Patty couldn't disguise her dismay. ''You don't love her!''

''How do you know that?''

''Anyone who sees the way you look at her can tell.'' Patty shook her head. ''Mark my words, Jack. One of these days when you least expect it, a woman is going to walk into your life and turn everything upside down. Think how horrible that moment will be for you if you're married to someone else.''

''Barbara's a good woman.''

Patty shrugged. ''She's all right, I guess. But if you choose her, you'll be settling. And you've never just settled for anything in your life.''

Jack didn't say anything.

Patty suddenly snapped her fingers. ''I almost forgot. Kevin wants me to invite you to a cookout at our house a week from Saturday. Are you free?''

Jack leaned forward and looked at his calendar. ''I'll be there.''

''You can even bring Barbara if you want,'' she said with a smile.

''I almost have to. If I come alone, you'll try to set me up with one of your friends.''

''I do tend to do that,'' Patty said apologetically. ''It's just that I love you and want to see you happy.'' Patty finished her drink and put it on the desk. ''I need some sleep, dear brother.''

Jack rose to his full height of six foot three. ''I'll

take you upstairs and tuck you in. Did you call Kevin to tell him where you are?''

''Before I came here.''

''You're lucky you fell in love with a writer who works at home.''

''Believe me, I give thanks every day for that man. I don't know what I'd do without him.''

''It goes both ways, Patty.''

She smiled up at her brother. ''That's the beauty of it.''

''Come on then, Dr. Phillips,'' he said as he gave her a hand up from the chair. ''Let's go.''

Moments later Jack stood at the window of his darkened apartment and stared outside. There was a restlessness in him that he couldn't shake. Was Patty right? Could the woman he'd unknowingly been searching for be out there somewhere?

Chapter 1

Riley Hennessey pressed the intercom button on his desk. "Has Kyra Courtland arrived yet?" he asked his secretary.

"She just walked through the door."

"Send her in."

Kyra was smiling at something the secretary said as she opened the door to her boss's office deep in the Department of Justice.

"What's she saying about me now?" he asked gruffly.

"Only that you're in a foul mood and I should just nod and agree with everything you say."

He pressed the intercom button again. "For the record, my dear Mrs. Henry, I am not in a foul mood."

"Yes, sir."

He waved Kyra into a seat across from his desk. He had to admit, even though he was fast approaching

sixty, he enjoyed looking at Kyra. She reminded him
of Grace Kelly, with her lovely face and soft blond
hair. But rather than being cool and aloof as her looks
might indicate, she was in fact a warm, wonderful
woman. It made a person feel good just to be in the
same room with her. And she carried herself with a
quiet dignity. Kyra worked in a world peopled mostly
by competitive men, and her warmth could have set
her up for harassment. But her dignity and humor had
won her co-workers' respect. Not one man at the department would have dreamed of making a pass at
her, no matter how tempting it might be. If anything,
they were protective of her the way they might have
been of a much beloved sister.

"What's so urgent that it couldn't wait until tomorrow?" Kyra asked with some evidence of that
good humor as she sank into the chair and crossed
her long legs.

"You're not going to like it."

"That much I already figured out."

Riley tossed his pen onto his desk as he leaned
back in his seat and propped up his feet. "I've got a
case I want you to look into."

"I'm listening."

"High-tech military hardware smuggling."

"To where?"

"Iran and China."

"What's that got to do with us?"

"All roads seem to lead from Washington—specifically a member of Congress and probably more
than one person at the Pentagon."

"It sounds as though you already know who."

"We have our suspicions. But that's not the same

as knowing it for a fact. Have you heard of a congressman by the name of Burton Banacomp?''

''Isn't he on the House Arms Committee?''

''That's the one. But we're getting ahead of ourselves. Let me give you some background. Do you know anything about how we dispose of our military hardware?''

''Not in any detail.''

''Every item manufactured for the Defense Department receives a code number. When it comes time to scrap the items because of obsolescence or downsizing in the military, these numbers are used to determine which pieces need to be destroyed before they're sold for scrap and which items, like refrigerators, can be sold as is. What's been happening is that some sensitive materiel—everything from rocket launchers to computers with nuclear launch codes still in memory—are being deliberately miscoded, shipped in crates labeling them as legitimate scrap and being sold to foreign countries that are potentially our enemies. You can imagine the repercussions for our national security.''

''This sounds more like a job for Customs than the Department of Justice.''

''Believe me, they're doing their part. We've been working with them and will continue to do so. But you and I both know that Customs inspects only about one-tenth of one percent of what leaves this country. We need to stop this flood at its source.''

''The source being...?''

''Mainly Washington. We've got someone on the inside at the Pentagon already who's managed to get some good information.''

"What about Burton's office?"

"He's a wily fellow. The people who are closest to Burton are all cronies—people he's known and trusted for years. Our efforts to get someone placed close to him haven't been at all successful."

"What about wiretaps?"

"We don't want to go that route. To get a tap means going to court and getting permission. Word might leak out and get back to the congressman. There are people all over this place who owe him favors. If that happens and he backs off, we'll never find out anything."

"This is all very interesting, Riley, but so far I don't see where I fit in."

Riley leaned back in his seat. "Let's say Banacomp is our man on the inside—and I believe he is. He has access to the codes, to the people who assign the codes and to the people who are supposed to destroy the coded equipment and sell it for scrap."

"Okay."

"What's missing in this picture?"

Kyra thought for a moment. "Well, if he intends to profit from selling the technology that hasn't been properly scrapped, he first has to own it, or at least have control over it."

"Exactly. And since he can't buy it himself when it's auctioned off, he has to have a middleman do it for him. What else?"

"He needs to be able to get it out of the country."

"Bingo."

"You sound as though you know how he's doing it."

"I do. Allessandro Shipping."

"That sounds familiar."

"It should. It's one of the largest international shipping companies in the world, and it's owned by Jack Allessandro, grandson of Tony Allessandro, who just happens to have been the head of the Chicago mob."

"But he's dead, isn't he?"

"Yeah, but Jack isn't."

"So you think the grandson is involved with the mob?"

"I don't have any concrete proof. He's been very careful in his business dealings to make everything look legitimate."

"And you've no doubt investigated every aspect of his life."

"Every corner."

"And you've come up with...?"

"Absolutely nothing."

"Then maybe you're on the wrong track," said Kyra.

"The mob thing might be a little far-fetched," he admitted, "although you have to wonder why he keeps his main offices in Chicago. It's not exactly famous for its international shipping. But that aside, Allessandro could be doing this on his own, without any mob input. My gut tells me that one way or another, he's involved. Allessandro and Banacomp knew each other as kids. They've remained good friends over the years. In fact, it was Banacomp's family who loaned Allessandro the money to get his business going. It's only logical that if Banacomp were trafficking in high-tech arms and information, he'd turn to his friend—who just happens to own a shipping company—for help in getting it out of the country."

"You're right. It makes sense."

"But?"

Kyra shook her head. "Something isn't right. Why would Jack Allessandro have to go to the Banacomps for a business loan? Why didn't he go to his grandfather, assuming Tony Allessandro was alive at the time."

"He was. From what I gather, there was some kind of falling-out between Jack and the old man. No one knows exactly what it was because the whole family is tight-lipped when it comes to anything personal. What we know is that after Jack's parents were murdered when he was eight, he was raised by his grandparents. When he was sixteen, he left home and cut himself off completely from his grandfather, though he kept in touch with his grandmother. When he was twenty-one, he went to court to get custody of his younger sister, Patty, and won, then raised her himself. The grandfather died of natural causes four years ago."

"That hardly sounds as though Jack is in cahoots with the mob. If anything, it would appear to be just the opposite."

"Maybe. Maybe not. Perhaps what repelled him as a youth attracts him as an adult."

Kyra chose not to pursue that angle. "What solid evidence do you have that Allessandro Shipping is involved?"

"None yet. Just gut instinct." Riley smiled. "That's where you come in."

Kyra waited.

"You're moving to Chicago for a while."

Kyra sat up straight. "You promised me that after the last time I wouldn't have to go undercover again."

"I know. And I meant it. But then this came up and you're the only one here I trust to take this on. You're perfect for it."

"Riley…"

"One of the places we think he's making major contacts is Spain. Most of the shipments of scrap that we've been able to trace go from the U.S. to Barcelona and from there to China and Iran. You're a whiz at languages. That puts you in a good position for getting information other investigators can't."

"And how do you intend to get me inside?"

"As it happens, Jack's going to be in need of a new assistant in a few days."

"Thanks to you, I presume?"

He grinned. "Let's just say we made his current assistant an offer she couldn't refuse."

"Meaning?"

"We found her the job of a lifetime and had a company quietly recruit her."

"And how do you know I'll get her job with Allessandro?"

"That's where you're on your own. There are only so many strings we can pull. If he doesn't like you, he won't hire you. And this guy won't hire you because you're pretty. He wants talent and reliability. I think he'd hire you on your résumé alone."

"You could make up a résumé like mine for someone else."

"Ah, but they wouldn't be able to back it up. Whoever we send in had better have the experience we say they have or Allessandro will fire them. You have what Allessandro wants just as you are.''

''So you'd be sending me in as myself?''

''More or less. Just without the Department of Justice credits.''

Kyra shook her head. ''I'm sorry, Riley, but I can't. I have Noah to think of. He's happy at our farm in Virginia. After all he's been through with the deaths of his parents, I don't want to uproot him again.''

''Your sister and her husband were killed over eighteen months ago, Kyra. Noah's just turned two. As far as he's concerned, you're his mother. In fact, legally speaking, you *are* his mother now. It won't be uprooting him at all if you're there.''

''Oh, Riley…''

''We've already picked out a house for you. It's in a really nice neighborhood with a park nearby. Lots of kids around for him to play with. Three bedrooms so you can take your aunt with you to watch Noah, just like she does now.''

''Even if I were to agree to this job, I certainly wouldn't want to involve my family. This is supposed to be an undercover assignment.''

''Well, there's a little problem with that.''

''I'm listening.''

''Believe me, Kyra, we've thought of all the downsides. We can only send you undercover to a certain extent. In other words, Jack Allessandro won't know that you work for the Department of Justice. Unfortunately, he'll have to know everything else. The reality is that when you travel with him, you might just come across someone who remembers you from the years you worked with your father when he was ambassador. It's not going to look good if Allessandro knows you by one name and someone greets you by another. It would ruin everything."

"I suppose that makes sense."

"And no one you run into will know you're with the Department of Justice because as far as the world is concerned, you've been working for Riley Hennessey—businessman, entrepreneur and one hell of a nice guy."

Kyra looked at him fondly for a long moment. "Don't you ever get tired of lying to people about who you really are? Don't you ever want to just stand up and shout to the world that you're not who they all think you are?"

"I used to, but I got over it." He moved around the desk and leaned against the edge, facing Kyra. "Honey, I know this is hard. But you have to look at the good we do. It's not lying for the sake of lying. We put the bad guys out of action. That alone makes it all worthwhile to me. So what do you say? Are you with me on this one?"

She apologized with her eyes. "I just can't."

"Okay, okay. We'll overlook your answer for now."

"Riley..."

He walked back around his desk, sat down and opened the voluminous file in front of him. "I've given you the basics already. This file will give you more details on the entire Allessandro family and the shipping company. Take it home with you and look it over. Your part in this would be strictly information gathering. As I said before, I don't want to do anything at this point that we'd need a judge for. Nothing can endanger this investigation. If Banacomp is dirty, I want to bring him down. If Jack Allessandro is conspiring with Banacomp to smuggle our technology and our arms into foreign countries that can then be turned on our own troops, I want them behind bars for as long as we can keep them there.''

Kyra sighed.

''If you decide to do this, you'll have a good shot at finding out things we can't from this end. And, remember, the closer you can get to him, the better it'll be.''

''What exactly does that mean?''

''Don't get all huffy on me, Kyra. Just try to make a friend out of Jack and his family. Get him to trust you so he'll confide things.''

There was a knock on the door.

''Come in,'' said Riley.

His secretary opened the door and smiled at Kyra. ''There's someone here to see you.''

Before the words were completely out, a little bundle of energy with bright blond hair came running into the office and into the arms of the woman he thought of as his mother. Kyra smiled as she hugged him. ''What are you doing here?''

He pointed a chubby little finger at an attractive woman standing in the doorway. ''Aunt Emiwy.'' He was a little hard to understand because his *l*'s sounded like *w*'s, but Kyra knew what he was saying. Actually, he was quite articulate for a two-year-old. She looked toward the door and smiled at her aunt. ''What a nice surprise.''

The woman, a fiftyish version of her niece, smiled back.

"Go home now," ordered Noah.

Kyra looked at Riley. "Are we finished here?"

But Riley was busy looking at Emily.

Kyra couldn't help smiling. "Riley? Hello?"

The man cleared his throat as he walked around his desk and lifted Noah high in his arms. "You're getting so big."

"Like my daddy," said Noah proudly. Kyra tried to keep the memory of Noah's parents alive with pictures. It warmed her heart that he mentioned his father now.

Riley kissed the child's cheek. Noah's father had worked for the Department of Justice. In fact, John was the one who had recruited Kyra. "Exactly like your dad."

Kyra was smiling, but there was sadness behind it. John had been killed by a car bomb—and her sister along with him. He'd been working on a case and gotten caught undercover. It had devastated Kyra. But it had also terrified her. To this day, she couldn't start a car without wincing, waiting for the explosion.

Riley put Noah down. "Yeah, I think we're finished. We'll go over things in more detail tomorrow, and then you need to head for Chicago to get that job. In addition to the phone in your home, you'll be issued a special cell phone for your calls to me. I want you to check in a minimum of once a week—more if you find anything interesting." He felt at ease speaking in front of Kyra's aunt. Emily was a good and trustworthy woman, one of the few people who knew what Kyra did for a living. Kyra had insisted on absolute honesty when her aunt had come to live with her.

"I haven't agreed to do it."

"A résumé has already been prepared and forwarded. They're interested. There's a number in the file I want you to call tomorrow so you can speak with a Miss Hanover, Allessandro's current assistant."

Kyra lifted a softly shaped eyebrow.

Riley was completely confident. "I know you won't turn me down."

"Do you see what I have to put up with when I come to work?" Kyra said to her aunt.

"It's a wonder you can face the day."

Kyra scooped up Noah in her arms. "Come on, little one. Let's go home." She looked at her aunt. "Did you bring your car?"

"No. You know how I hate driving in the city."

They started to leave, but Riley called out and stopped them. Walking up to Kyra, he tucked the Allessandro file under her arm. "Can't forget that."

"You don't quit, do you?" she asked.

"Never. Have a nice afternoon, ladies...and gentleman."

They left the office and walked to Kyra's Jeep Grand Cherokee. While her aunt climbed into the passenger seat, Kyra fastened Noah into his car seat, then climbed behind the wheel.

"So what kind of assignment was Riley trying to talk you into?"

"One that would involve the three of us moving to Chicago for a few months."

"That wouldn't be so bad. Especially if it's only for a short time. Would you be keeping the farm?"

"Yes. The house in Chicago would be rented."

"Well, as long as I can count on coming back home, I suppose it's all right." She touched her niece's arm. "You know I'll stay with you wherever you go for however long you need me."

Kyra leaned over the console and hugged her. "I don't know what I would have done if you hadn't shown up when Noah came to live with me."

"It goes both ways, dear. After my husband died, I was completely at loose ends. You and Noah saved me from unbearable loneliness."

"You'll always have a home with us."

"Well, at least until you marry."

"That isn't going to happen," said Kyra as she straightened and turned the key in the ignition.

"Of course it will. You're young and beautiful. Someday a man will come along who sweeps you off your feet."

"I'm unsweepable."

Emily smiled. "I know that's what you believe now, but it will happen."

"I might say the same about you. If anyone should be able to find love again, it's you."

"At my age?"

"You're not even sixty yet!"

"I will be in five years."

"So now you're telling me there's an age limit?"

"Passion is best left to the young. I think I'd find the emotional upheaval too exhausting. I rather like things the way they are."

"Then we're the perfect couple."

"This Chicago job..." said Emily as Kyra put the car into gear. "Is it dangerous?"

"Not particularly. It's just a matter of information gathering."

"I wish you'd get into a different line of work."

"I know you do," said Kyra gently. "I'm trying to get a full-time desk job."

"You'll hate that."

"Not at all. I'm looking forward to it. I don't like being away from Noah."

"Noah is fine. You see him as much as most working mothers see their children. And he has the advantage of not having to be put in a day-care facility."

Kyra looked at her aunt and smiled. "As long as he has both of us, I know he'll do well."

"What do you think you'll decide about Chicago?"

Kyra was silent for a moment. "I'm not going to go. I'm absolutely not going to go."

Chapter 2

Well, here she was, Kyra thought as she looked around the elegant offices of Allessandro Shipping through the slender octagon-shaped eye glasses she'd chosen to wear instead of her contacts. Right where she swore she wouldn't be.

A man walked past her chair and stopped at the receptionist's desk. "Good morning, Kim."

The young woman smiled up at him—beamed up at him, actually. "Mr. Chesler! Good morning."

Kyra did a quick mental check. Chesler. Barry Chesler. Vice president of Allessandro Shipping. Childhood friend of Jack Allessandro and Congressman Banacomp. Early thirties. And as Kyra watched the tall blond man with the wide smile, she conceded his file pictures didn't do him justice. He was much more handsome in person.

"What can I do for you this morning?" asked the receptionist.

"Hold my calls. I don't want to be disturbed."

"Yes, sir."

"Is Jack in?"

"Yes, but..." She lowered her voice so Kyra couldn't hear the rest of what was being said.

The man turned to Kyra and hit her with the full wattage of his smile. "So you're the face behind the résumé I've been hearing so much about from Jack's assistant."

As Kyra rose from her seat, he shook her hand. "I'm Barry Chesler, vice president."

"Nice to meet you."

He waved her back into her seat and sat across from her. "I don't think I'm giving anything away if I tell you that it's between you and one other woman who was interviewed yesterday."

"It's a good job. I assumed I wasn't the only one who applied."

"I understand your father was an ambassador."

"That's right."

"To what country?"

"Spain."

"And you were with him during some of that time?"

"Yes."

"Then you must have met the diplomat Francisco Perez at one time or another."

Kyra knew exactly who he was talking about. "And his wife, Maria Paz. The last time I saw them was about five years ago."

"They're both good friends of mine."

"Then you're lucky. They're nice people."

His smile grew even wider, if that was possible.

Kyra felt as though she had just passed some kind of test.

"If you do get hired, you'll be doing some work for me, as well. Not a lot, though. My duties don't really require a full-time secretary. And Kim usually takes care of my mail."

"That's not a problem."

"Well," he said as he rose, "excuse me. I have things to do. Good luck with your interview."

"Thank you."

With a wink at the receptionist, he walked through a door just behind the reception area.

"Miss Courtland?" said the receptionist. "Mr. Allessandro's assistant will see you now."

"Thank you," Kyra said, rising.

The receptionist rose and opened the same door Barry Chesler had gone through.

The office was large and full of light from the big windows that looked out on Chicago. An elegant woman in her early thirties rose from behind her desk to greet Kyra with an extended hand. "How do you do, Miss Courtland? Thank you for coming. I'm Eleanor Hanover."

"It's nice to meet you," said Kyra.

The assistant looked Kyra over carefully, from her conservatively but elegantly suited figure to the blond hair she wore pulled away from her face in a simple French twist. "As I told you on the telephone yesterday, Mr. Allessandro and I went over your résumé and were both pleased with what we saw. Before making a commitment, though, we wanted to meet you in person. Now that I have, I can honestly say—for my part at least—that you're exactly what we're looking for. Your previous employer," she said as she checked a paper on her desk, "Mr. Riley Hennessey—" she looked back at Kyra "—couldn't say enough complimentary things about you. Clearly he wishes you were staying in Virginia."

"I enjoyed working with him, as well."

"Why did you decide to move to the Chicago area?"

"I spent a lot of time in the Midwest as a child and have always loved it. I've thought about returning for years, but the time didn't seem right until now."

She nodded. "I know what you mean. I'm going to miss it myself."

"Where will you be going?"

"New York. An opportunity arose that I simply couldn't pass up."

"I guess the timing is right for both of us."

"Yes and no," said the woman as she shuffled through several pages and then perused the one she'd been looking for. "I have to start my new job sooner than I expected, so whoever we hire is going to be on her own almost immediately." She continued to scan the document. "We discussed, of course, that you'll be required to do quite a bit of traveling with Mr. Allessandro. Are you sure that won't pose a problem with the care of your son?"

"I have an aunt who lives with me and takes care of him when I'm not there."

"That will work out nicely then. And you'll need to make sure your passport is in order."

"It is."

"Lovely. I've made some notes on things you'll need to know in order to ease yourself into this job—that is, of course, if Mr. Allessandro approves of you.''

''What's he like?''

The woman closed the file and looked at Kyra. ''He's very smart and can be a little intimidating at times. He expects things to be done correctly the first time and has very little patience with mistakes or stupid questions.''

''I see.''

''Look, I shouldn't say this, but I like you and I think you're probably going to get the job. If you have any designs on attracting his personal attention, forget it. I've been here for five years and in all of that time, he's never made so much as an off-color remark in my presence, much less anything resembling a pickup line.''

Kyra smiled. ''At least it's a safe working environment.''

''He's an interesting man. I can't honestly say I know him all that personally, though. I don't think even the women he dates know him. He tends to hold himself aloof from everyone. Just remember not to take it personally.''

''I don't need to be friends with him. I just want to work.''

''Then you won't be disappointed.'' She pushed back her chair. ''And that's all the gossip you're going to get from me. All that's left now is for you to meet Mr. Allessandro.''

Kyra was a little nervous, but did her best not to show it. ''I'm ready.''

''Just remember that his bark is worse than his bite. If you do your job well, the two of you will get along

fine.'' She pressed the intercom button. ''Mr. Allessandro?''

''Yes?''

''Ms. Courtland is here to meet you.''

''Bring her in.''

Kyra adjusted her glasses as she rose and followed
the woman through the connecting door to another
office.

It was a very masculine room with rich wood and
leather, bright with sunshine that streamed in through
a panel of windows. But Kyra's attention was completely focused on the man behind the heavy desk.
He was dressed in a dark suit, white shirt and striped
tie. No gaudy splashes of color for this man.

His dark hair was thick and well-groomed with a
hint of gray at the temples. He looked at Kyra with
unsmiling dark blue eyes as he rose from his chair
and stretched out his hand.

''How do you do?'' she said, giving it a firm shake.

He waved her into a chair across from his desk, his
eyes on her all the while, seemingly missing nothing.
''Excuse us, Ms. Hanover.''

''Buzz me if you want anything,'' she said as she
closed the door behind her.

Jack looked at the woman seated across from him.
Even with her hair pulled back and the glasses, he
could see she was lovely. And he liked her handshake. Firm and sure. ''So tell me, Ms. Courtland,
why do you want to work for me?''

''I like the job description, particularly the travel.
You're based in Chicago, which is where I want to
be. You have good benefits, and I think I have a future with your company.''

Jack was expressionless as he watched her. "I understand you have a son. Are you married?"

"No."

"Divorced?"

"No."

"I see. Will your responsibilities at home with the child interfere with your work here?"

"As I already told your assistant, not at all."

"If they do, you're out."

"I understand."

"Good. I also note from your résumé that your late father was at one time an ambassador."

"Yes, he was."

"And you acted as his hostess?"

"Frequently, after my mother died."

"That ties in to what you'll be doing for me more often than not. Along with the travel, I'm required to do a great deal of entertaining. Since I'm not married myself, the function of hostess is one my assistant is expected to carry out, as well as overseeing the general arrangements for dinners."

"I'm quite used to doing things of that nature."

"It says on your résumé that you speak Italian and Spanish."

"That's right."

"*¿Habla usted la lengua muy bien a salamente un voco?*" Jack asked.

"*Habla muy bien porque aprendi de niña,*" Kyra responded easily.

"If you want the job, it's yours."

"I do."

"Good."

Kyra smiled. "Thank you."

There was no return smile. "You understand that time is short. Ms. Hanover is leaving tomorrow. That means I'll need you to start first thing in the morning."

"I'll be here."

He leaned back in his chair, his eyes on hers. "Is there anything you'd like to ask me?"

"Will there be any problem in getting my son included in my medical coverage?"

"No. I had Ms. Hanover check on that this morning."

Kyra couldn't believe he'd thought to do that. She was impressed. "Thank you."

"Anything else?"

"Not at the moment."

He leaned forward and picked up a pen. "Then I'll see you in the morning at nine."

Kyra knew when she'd been dismissed. Without saying anything else, she rose and left the office, closing the door quietly behind her.

Eleanor Hanover looked at her with a quizzically raised brow.

"I start tomorrow."

She gave a knowing nod. "I had a feeling you'd be the one he'd choose." She looked at the stack of papers on her desk. "Is there anywhere you need to be right now?"

"No."

"Good." She pointed at a chair. "Let's do some preliminary work so you have at least a general idea of the layout here and some of your duties before you get tossed in the deep end."

"I'd appreciate that."

"I want the transition to go as smoothly as possible."

"Believe me, so do I."

"Then let's get to work."

And work they did. For hours. Eleanor took her through things one time only and Kyra took notes, paying particular attention to anything that involved security, such as the fact that there were no cameras in any of the executive or secretarial offices. Jack Allessandro apparently didn't like to feel as though he was being watched. That would make Kyra's work a lot easier. And she also listened carefully to anything that would help her get information out of the computer system.

It wasn't going to be easy. There was a main password that would get her into the system and allow access to certain files, but there were different security levels for different users. Obviously the top brass at the company, like Jack Allessandro and Barry Chesler, had access to everything but each other's personal files. Eleanor's security level was restricted to files she needed, but nothing more. That would be Kyra's lot.

The trick would be getting into Jack's files.

She was going to need help for that. While she was competent at using computers, she was no whiz.

She kept listening and taking notes.

Jack Allessandro came and went several times. He spoke to Eleanor, always calling her Ms. Hanover. After acknowledging Kyra's presence with the briefest of nods, he behaved as though she wasn't there.

Eleanor also took her around the company and introduced her to dozens of people. Kyra couldn't begin to keep track of the names, but she knew they were all on a roster of the company that she had in her files at home.

Eleanor seemed to know what Kyra was thinking. "Don't worry if you can't put the names with the faces right away. Your office is fairly isolated. When Mr. Allessandro wants to talk to anyone, he usually goes to them rather than having them come to him."

"Good."

As they walked through the corridors, warm with rich woods, Kyra checked out the security cameras.

She couldn't be positive, but she thought they were located behind beautifully carved boxes that were strategically placed high on the walls and appeared to be works of art.

The offices were absolutely beautiful Kyra noted.

"The art," explained Eleanor, pointing out the exquisite paintings that lined the walls, "was collected from all over the world, chosen by the employees. It belongs to all of us."

"How is that?"

"Each employee gets a painting after they've been here for ten years."

"How do they decide which painting?"

"It's a lottery system. That's the only fair way to do it."

That was something that hadn't been in the file. But Kyra knew that while Allessandro was a privately held corporation, the employees all participated in profit sharing, from the executives to the janitors to the ship workers.

Was a man who set up a corporation like that the kind of man who would smuggle arms?

Riley certainly thought so.

And Riley was never wrong.

"Let's go to the lobby," said Eleanor.

They took the elevator to the ground floor. Eleanor took her to the circular desk where the security guard sat surrounded by small television monitors. Eleanor smiled at him. "Sam, this is Kyra Courtland. She'll be Mr. Allessandro's new assistant as of tomorrow."

The middle-aged guard rose and shook Kyra's hand. "Nice to meet you, miss. If you have any problems or questions, just ask any one of us on duty."

"Thank you." Kyra looked at the monitors and noticed that each one changed every five seconds to a view from a different camera.

Eleanor took her arm and led Kyra back to the elevator. "You came in through the lobby this morning, but starting tomorrow you'll be parking in the garage." She pressed the garage button and was quiet until the doors opened. "That's my car," she said, pointing to a red sports car one parking space away. "That'll be where you park tomorrow. To get upstairs from here, you'll need a key card." She pulled one out of her pocket as they stepped back onto the elevator and inserted it, then pressed the floor number of their office before removing the card. "You might as well take this one," she said, handing it to Kyra. "I won't have any use for it. If you forget to bring it, you'll have to go in through the lobby. And if you come in on weekends or come back to the office at night, the elevator automatically stops at the lobby level. You'll have to check in with the guard. He'll then unlock the elevator so it can continue to the office."

"All right." Kyra noticed a second key card slot on the panel. "What's this for?"

"Mr. Allessandro's apartment. It's on the top floor of the building. He has a separate key card for that." She looked at her watch. "We'd better get back to the office. There's still a lot I need to show you before the end of the day."

And there was.

Kyra absorbed everything she was told and then some.

Toward the end of the day, Barry strolled casually out of Jack's office and sat on the edge of Eleanor's desk. "I understand congratulations are in order," he said to Kyra.

"Thank you."

"I'm glad Jack decided on you. You're much prettier than the other candidate."

"Barry!" said Eleanor in a tone meant to be chastising, but which was really a little flirtatious.

"Forget I said that." He smiled at Kyra. "Anyway, welcome to Allessandro Shipping. I hope you like it here."

"I'm sure I will."

"And you," he said, turning to Eleanor, "are going to meet me for a last drink after work. I'm going to miss our evening cocktails. It's been a ritual I've looked forward to every Tuesday since you started working here."

"I'll miss it, too."

"Don't forget."

"I never have."

Kyra watched as Barry walked out the door and closed it behind him. "He's a lot different from Mr.

Allessandro," she said, more to herself than to Eleanor.

"A lot."

"Are you and he...?" Kyra let the unfinished question hang in the air.

Eleanor wasn't the least bit embarrassed. "We used to be occasional lovers. Nothing serious. Besides, he's married. I knew it wasn't going to go anywhere. If there's one thing I've learned over the years, it's that men don't mind a little intimate flirtation on the side, but don't expect them to leave their wives. They won't do it. It's too expensive." She sighed. "He is gorgeous, though, isn't he?"

Kyra had to admit that he was. But that wasn't what she was thinking about. "I didn't see Barry go into Mr. Allessandro's office. How did he get in there?"

"They have connecting doors."

"Oh." She put her notebook on the desk. "They seem such an odd couple."

Eleanor nodded. "I know what you mean. Completely different personalities. But that's why they work so well together. Jack has the brains and business know-how to come up with the deals, and Barry has the charm to put them over."

"Then why is Barry only a vice president?"

"Make no mistake. This is Jack Allessandro's company. But Barry gets paid plenty for his trouble."

Kyra smiled.

"What?" asked Eleanor.

"I think I'm going to like working here."

"Any reason in particular?"

"Interesting people. Very interesting people."

Chapter 3

Kyra had been awake for a few minutes without actually realizing it. It was odd how some of her dreams gradually turned into thoughts so that going from being asleep to awake was barely noticeable. She stretched her arms high over her head, then put on her glasses and focused on the bedside clock.

That couldn't be right.

She blinked and refocused.

"Oh my God!" she yelled as she flew out of bed and began pulling off her T-shirt and hopping on first one foot and then the other, stripping out of her boxers and leaving a trail of clothes that followed her into the shower.

She was in and out within five minutes, dragged a brush across her teeth, jammed her makeup into her purse, indiscriminately pulled a suit skirt and jacket off the hangers and zipped and buttoned herself into them, shouldered her purse and carried her high heels as she raced out of her room.

Her aunt walked into the living room, wearing her robe and slippers, and looked at Kyra in surprise. "What are you still doing here?"

"I overslept! My first day and I overslept!"

The older woman hurried toward the kitchen. "At least let me get you some juice. Maybe a slice of toast."

Kyra kissed her cheek. "Thanks, but I don't have the time. Is Noah still sleeping?"

"You let him stay up too late last night."

"I know, but we were having such a nice time playing. And I hadn't seen him all day. I'll just give him a kiss goodbye."

Kyra tiptoed quietly into her son's room and leaned over his crib. He was lying on his tummy in the kind of deep sleep only a child was capable of, his even breaths floating on the otherwise still air. She pushed his damp hair away from his face before kissing him on his sleep-warmed cheek. "I love you," she whispered.

Noah didn't stir.

Kyra carefully pulled his blanket up a little higher and kissed him one more time before tiptoeing out of his room and pulling the door partially closed.

"Gotta go," she called in her best loud whisper to her aunt as she sprinted for the front door.

"What time will you be home?"

"Six-thirty. Seven. If it's any later, I'll call."

Kyra jumped into her green Jeep, tossed her purse and her shoes onto the passenger seat, revved the engine with a stockinged foot and took off through the suburban streets at a speed considerably above the legal limit.

Reaching for her purse, she felt her way through its contents for her makeup and put it on as best she could whenever she was stopped in traffic or caught at a red light.

Her hair was a little trickier. It took two hands and the lights didn't last long enough to finish the job.

Forty minutes later, after fighting traffic she might have missed had she left home a little earlier, Kyra pulled into the underground parking garage, found her reserved spot near the elevators and sat there while she quickly finished her hair and put on her shoes.

Pushing her glasses up the bridge of her nose, Kyra gave herself a quick check in the rearview mirror. Not great, but not too bad, all things considered.

Kyra quickly made her way to the express elevator, pressed the button for the twentieth floor and fidgeted for the few seconds it took the elevator to get there.

When the doors opened, she rushed down the hall into the main offices, said good morning to Kim, went into her own office and sank, exhausted, into the chair behind her desk.

Her intercom buzzed.

"Yes?" she said as she pressed the button.

"You're late," said Jack Allessandro.

Kyra let out a long breath. "Yes, I am. I overslept. It won't happen again."

"See that it doesn't. I'm expecting Constantine Zukos in five minutes. Show him into my office, then sit in on the meeting and take notes."

"Yes, sir."

No sooner had she pulled a notebook out of her

desk drawer than Kim buzzed to tell her that the man had arrived.

Kyra went to the door, opened it and smiled at the short, swarthy-skinned Greek. "Hello, Mr. Zukos. I'm Kyra Courtland, Mr. Allessandro's assistant. May I get you coffee? Tea?"

"No, thank you," he said pleasantly in a thick accent.

"Come with me then."

She showed him into Jack's office, then sat inconspicuously to one side with the notebook on her lap.

Kyra had always been a people watcher. She liked to examine facial expressions, body language, tone of voice and try to figure out what was really going on versus what was being said.

And her instincts were usually right. That was one of the qualities that made her so good at her job.

She used that skill now.

Jack Allessandro, she noted, never smiled. Not when he greeted the man and not during their conversation. His questions were specific and to the point. It was obvious that he had a piercing intelligence.

But not much warmth or charm.

The Greek clearly wanted to do business with Allessandro Shipping. Kyra took occasional notes, but not many.

At one point, Jack looked directly at her as if to ask why she wasn't writing more down. She looked right back at him, unintimidated.

Seemingly.

She knew just from the brief time she'd spent with Jack Allessandro that this was one man she wouldn't

want to have angry with her. There was no question
in her mind that his still waters ran very deep indeed.

Still, she listened and watched more than she wrote.

She had decided after just a few minutes that Constantine Zukos wasn't a man to be trusted. If she
owned Allessandro Shipping, she wouldn't even let
him onto the property, much less buy used freighters
from him.

Jack ended their conversation abruptly and rose
from behind his desk to indicate that the meeting was
over. The two men shook hands, then Jack showed
him to the door.

Kyra rose and would have followed the Greek out,
but Jack closed the door as soon as Zukos had gone,
blocking Kyra's exit. "Sit down," he ordered.

Kyra knew from his tone that she was in trouble.
She sat.

"I told you specifically that I wanted you in here
to take notes." He moved to stand directly in front
of her and took the nearly blank notepad from her
hands. "Where are they?"

"I didn't see the need to write much down."

"Why not?"

"Because my intention was—and is—to go to my
computer and type up the important points that were
made by both of you."

"Which you remember without having to take
notes?" he asked skeptically.

"That's right. Besides, I don't think you're going
to do business with him."

"And why would you think that?"

"You don't like him. Neither did I."

"I do business with a lot of people I don't like."

"Ah, but not with people you don't trust."

"You think I don't trust Zukos?"

"If you do, you shouldn't."

Jack half sat, half leaned on the edge of his desk, his arms folded across his chest, his piercing blue gaze clearly showing interest in what she had to say. "Why?"

"He's hiding something. Whether it's about the freighters he's trying to unload on you or his business in general, I don't know. But something isn't right."

"And how did you come to this conclusion, Ms. Courtland? You know nothing about the man except what you saw and heard in this office for fifteen minutes."

"I knew he wasn't to be trusted after five minutes."

Jack lifted a skeptical eyebrow.

"Woman's intuition. I'm sure you've heard of it."

"Of course. But I've never been confronted with such a shining example," he said dryly. "So tell me, Ms. Courtland, what things did this woman's intuition of yours think were of note?"

"Did you notice that when you asked him direct questions about his freighters, he fidgeted with his fingers and answered without looking you in the eye?"

"I can't say that I did."

"And he found it necessary to name-drop in order to impress you."

"Lots of people do that."

"Not those who are really close to the people whose names they're dropping. I think he figures that

the names will give him a certain cachet in your eyes
and you won't check out his credentials."

Jack was finding this interesting. "What else?"

Kyra found herself staring at him. His expression
was no longer skeptical and his eyes had actually
warmed a little.

He was the most remarkably attractive man....

"Ms. Courtland?"

Kyra's own eyes widened when she realized she
was staring. She cleared her throat. "Also, I found
his overall demeanor toward you too deferential."

"You think that's a bad thing?"

"Considering he came in here posing as an
equal—yes, I do." Kyra rose, notepad in hand.

"Is that it?" he asked.

"Yes."

Jack just looked at her.

Kyra stood her ground. "If I've overstepped my
bounds in what I've said, I apologize, but sometimes
second opinions help in making decisions."

Still he said nothing.

Kyra wanted to run through the door but stayed
where she was. "If you'd rather I didn't express myself about these things, tell me and I won't do it again.
Otherwise, I'll just type up the notes." She started to
leave.

Jack reached out and caught her arm to hold her in
place. "Just a minute."

Kyra was very aware of his hand on her arm—and
very aware when he took it away.

"Follow up on your hunches and see what you
find."

"Yes, sir." Even though he remained leaning against his desk, she still had to look up at him.

"Did you do this kind of thing with your last employer?"

"Frequently."

"And what was his opinion of your observations?"

"I believe he came to value them."

"Were you always right?"

"Almost always."

He inclined his head toward her notepad. "When you type your rather sparse written notes, add the thoughts that you've expressed. Let's see exactly how accurate you are."

"All right." Without waiting for anything further, she turned to open the door and nearly bumped into a young man getting ready to enter. "Excuse me," he said.

Kyra knew he was Jack Allessandro's cousin because she'd seen his picture in a file. He was dark, like Jack, but not quite as tall.

And he had an attitude.

She could tell just by looking at him. Even when he was still, he seemed to swagger. He was very, very sure of himself.

He took a step back and eyed Kyra up and down.

Rather than taking offense, Kyra found it amusing and stood absolutely still while he completed his visual journey.

"You must be Jack's new assistant," he said, a little Elvis-like curl turning up one corner of his mouth.

"That's right."

"Lose the glasses."

"I beg your pardon?"

"You're a beautiful woman. The glasses are stylish but they detract."

Kyra didn't miss a beat. "Lose the attitude."

If nothing else, she succeeded in shocking him. "What?"

"You're a handsome man. The attitude detracts."

A genuine smile curved his mouth. "Whoa! Nice one. What's your name?"

"Kyra Courtland," she responded politely.

"I'm Carl Allessandro. Is my cousin working you too hard?"

"Not so far."

"Let me know if he does. I pride myself on the speedy rescue of damsels in distress."

"Based on our short acquaintance, I'd say that's like jumping from the frying pan into the fire."

"Yeah, well, my offer still stands."

"Carl," Jack said without any sign of amusement at their banter, "I need to talk to you now."

Carl looked at Kyra and rolled his eyes as he walked past her.

Kyra left the door slightly ajar as she went to her desk. A moment later there was a firm click. Either Carl or Jack had closed it the rest of the way.

Carl sat in the chair across from his cousin and raised his feet to rest on the desk. "I like your new assistant. She's got spunk."

"Admire her on your own time."

"Meaning she isn't off-limits?"

"Her limits are whatever she sets, although somehow I don't think you're her type." He knocked Carl's feet off the desk, then leaned back in his chair and looked at his cousin long and hard. "Where have you been for the past week?"

"I took a little vacation."

"You left with no notice. No one knew where you were, what you were doing or when you'd be back."

Carl shrugged. "I needed to get away."

"From what? It's not like you're overworked—even when you bother to show up."

"Excuse me, cousin, but I've brought in a hell of a lot of business over the past six months."

"Three new accounts. That's what you've accomplished."

Carl sighed. "Selling space on freighters. Do you have any idea how boring that is? Give me something interesting to do and I'll be the best worker you've got, believe me."

"You have a stake in this business, Carl. I gave you stock. The more money the company earns, the more you earn. Maybe it isn't always interesting, but it's work that needs to be done. I did it for years when I started this business. I still do it."

"Yeah, well—"

"Look, Carl, I didn't want to hire you. You know that. I did it as a favor to our grandmother." He leaned forward to emphasize his next point. "But don't think that I won't fire you. If you disappear like that again, don't bother coming back."

Carl looked at his cousin with scarcely concealed dislike. "You wouldn't dare."

"You want to bet your job on it?" Jack asked evenly.

"We'll see what Grandmother has to say about that."

"This is my company, Carl. No one tells me how to run it. I've let you get away with a lot of things I wouldn't tolerate from others because you're family, but no more. One more disappearing act and you're gone for good."

Carl rose. "Are you finished?"

"For now."

Carl opened the door to Kyra's office and walked past her without speaking, his mouth an angry straight line.

She made a mental note that he might be someone she should try to get closer to as the weeks went by. He was rather low on the company directory, but he was family and he clearly wasn't too thrilled with Cousin Jack. Carl just might know some things. And if he got mad enough, he might even be willing to talk.

Jack walked out of his office with some papers that he put on the desk in front of her. "I'm giving a business dinner for eight men here at the office on Thursday evening at seven o'clock," he said as he leaned over her, his chest pressing her shoulder as he put check marks beside some of the names on the paper. "Specifically these men."

Kyra closed her eyes and took a deep breath. He smelled wonderful. She couldn't describe it. Just good. Clean.

"I'd like you to make the arrangements and act as hostess."

As he straightened away from her, Kyra reached for her right shoulder, still warm from the pressure of his chest, and rested her fingers there.

"Are you following this?" he asked when she didn't respond.

"Yes, of course." She looked up at him. "Hostess in what capacity?"

"I want you to greet them, make small talk during the before-dinner drinks, sit at the table with us to make sure no one is in need of anything, take mental notes and see them to the door when they leave."

"Do you have any specific instructions with regard to the kind of meal?"

"Just do a good job. The countries they're from are listed next to their names. Make sure there's nothing on the menu that offends any of them. One account in particular could be worth millions of business annually." He leaned over her again, this time brushing against her fingers, and turned one of the checks into an *x*. "Take special care of this one."

"Yes, sir."

"If anyone gets out of line with you, come to me and I'll take care of it."

Kyra looked up at Jack. "Does that happen often?"

"No." His eyes moved slowly over her face. "But you're very attractive and any man, after a few drinks, might forget his manners."

Somehow she knew that Jack Allessandro wasn't one of them. He would never drink enough to make him forget his manners. He struck Kyra as the kind of man who was in complete control of himself at all times.

"Any questions?" he asked, still looking at her.

He was an absolutely remarkable-looking man.

"Ms. Courtland?"

Her eyes widened as she realized she'd completely

missed what he'd said. "I'm sorry. I stopped tracking for a moment. What did you say?"

"I asked if you had any questions."

"No. Not at the moment."

"Let me know when you do. I'd rather have you ask me questions now than make stupid mistakes later."

She nodded.

When Jack walked back into his office, Kyra rose from her desk and went to the windows to stare outside.

It was a beautiful summer day but she felt a chill.

She was startled by the sudden and unexpected realization that she was attracted to Jack Allessandro.

Very attracted.

This was a man she was investigating. There was supposed to be a certain amount of detachment involved in that. There always had been before.

But Jack was different.

Her reaction to him was different.

Now that she was aware of that, she could deal with it like the professional investigator she was.

There wasn't a doubt in Kyra's mind that she could handle Jack.

If this man was a criminal, she was going to put him away.

In the meantime, she would make herself indispensable to him. Walking back to her desk, Kyra immediately pulled up the information she'd put on the computer about his likes and dislikes. Eleanor had left a list of caterers. She made the necessary phone calls, planned the menu with enough variety that even the most finicky eaters would be satisfied and none offended, selected the wines and arranged for servers—and all before the end of the business day.

As she was cleaning off her desk and getting ready to leave for the evening, a woman swept in and kept on going right past her and into Jack's office.

Kyra sprang to her feet and gave chase. "Excuse me!"

Jack was on the phone. When he saw the woman walk in, he didn't look exactly happy to see her. Not unhappy, just not happy. "I'll get back to you," he said to the person at the other end of the line, then hung up.

"I'm sorry, Mr. Allessandro," Kyra said from the doorway.

Jack stood. "Ms. Wendt," he began, sounding reluctant to make the introduction. He no doubt felt that this was mixing business with his personal life. "This is my new assistant." He didn't even use Kyra's name. She felt duly put in her place.

The woman was sleek and stunning. She could easily have been a model. Her short, pixie-style hair was incredibly red and set off her wide-set gray eyes and pale, flawless skin. She was very tall—nearly six feet—and elegant in the effortless sort of way that sometimes was a natural part of being that tall.

The woman looked Kyra over and apparently decided she wasn't a threat she needed to concern herself with. "Hello," she said dismissively, turning her head away before the word was even out of her mouth.

Kyra inclined her head. "Excuse me. I'll be going home now unless you need me for something."

"Go on," said Jack. "I'll be out of the office all

day tomorrow, but I'll be back in time for the dinner."

"All right. Good night." After closing the door, Kyra stood there for a moment. She shouldn't have been surprised by Jack's taste in women, and yet she was. Physically they were very nearly perfectly matched. He was coolly handsome; she was coolly beautiful. They both seemed to have a certain aloof arrogance.

She found herself trying to imagine them making love.

Where had that come from?

And yet it was there.

Kyra shook her head in an effort to clear her thoughts. Where and with whom Jack Allessandro spent his nights was none of her business.

When Kyra got to her car, she pulled out her cell phone and pressed Riley's number. He answered on the first ring.

"Hi, Riley. It's me."

"Hey, kid. What's happening?"

"I need you to look someone up for me."

"Sure."

"Constantine Zukos. He's in shipping. He was in here today, trying to unload some freighters onto Allessandro."

"What do you want to know?"

"I'd like a detailed background check. See if anything stands out."

"When do you need it?"

"As soon as you have it. You can fax it to me at home."

"Will do. I'll get someone on it right away."

"Thanks."

"Anything interesting happening?"

"Lots, but I don't know what to do with any of it yet."

"What kind of access do you have to the computer files?"

"Very limited. But I haven't had any time to experiment. The job keeps me busy."

"You're going to have to make time. We need to get this investigation going."

"I know that, Riley," she said impatiently.

"Work nights, when no one else is around."

"I don't really want to be picked up on security cameras at this point. Just let me handle it. I always get the job done, don't I?"

"Always. I guess I'm a little anxious about this case. I don't want to see another shipment get through."

"I know. But one just might. This is going to take time. Maybe months."

"I'll back off." He changed the subject. "How's the house?"

"Little, with a tiny yard."

"But nice?"

"It's all right. I mean, we've only been in it for two days."

"How's the furniture?"

"It's fine." Kyra grew quiet.

"What is it?" Riley asked.

"Would you check two other people for me?"

"Sure."

"Carl Allessandro and Barry Chesler."

"We have files on them already, just as we do the rest of the employees there."

"But they're sketchy. I mean really check them. I want to know everything there is to know about them. Check them as thoroughly as you did Jack and his family."

"All right. That'll take a while."

"I know. There's a dinner tomorrow night with some business types. I'll find out what I can there and send you a report when it's ready."

"Good. I had a computer installed at your place today with a direct hookup to my computer, along with a scanner. Send me whatever you get as soon as you get it."

"I will. Thanks, Riley. And just one more thing. I'll need an updated password finder disk."

"I'll Express Mail it to you tonight."

"Thanks."

"Anything else? I mean, if you want high-tech, I'll get you high-tech."

"Let's see what I can get on my own first."

"Fair enough. Bye for now, kid."

Kyra touched the power button to disconnect the call and dropped the phone into her purse.

Before she could start her car, Jack and The Wendt Woman stepped out of the garage elevator. Kyra watched as they walked away from her. Suddenly the woman stopped. Jack turned toward her. The woman put her arms around his neck and drew his face to hers. His arms went around the woman and pulled her body closer to his as their lips met.

Kyra shifted uncomfortably in her seat, wishing she

were anywhere but where she was—and yet unable to look away.

As Jack raised his head, he looked straight into Kyra's eyes.

Neither of them looked away.

And then in one fluid movement, he turned away from Kyra, put his arm around the woman's waist and guided her toward his car.

Kyra started her own car and accelerated out of her parking space, past Jack and the woman and out of the garage.

She wasn't upset.

She wasn't.

It had nothing to do with her.

The drive home seemed to take forever.

It had been a long day and she wanted to get home to Noah.

She turned on the radio, changed the stations until she listened to ten of them for all of five seconds each and turned it off again.

There was silence except for the purr of the engine.

Kyra wished she were back in Virginia. She had a bad feeling about this assignment. Her instincts had told her from the first moment that she should turn it down.

It wasn't like her to go against her instincts.

That was another of the qualities that made her good at what she did.

And yet, here she was.

All of her second-guessing disappeared, though, when she pulled into the driveway and saw Noah climb off his bright red tricycle to run to her.

She met him halfway and lifted him high in the air.

And when he wrapped his little arms around her neck to hug her, Kyra pushed work from her mind. She smiled at her aunt, who was sitting on the steps of the small porch.

Everything would be all right.

Jack lay in bed on his back, his arm behind his head, and listened to the even breaths of the woman sleeping beside him.

He couldn't relax.

Climbing out of bed, he went into Barbara's bathroom and took a hot shower. With a towel wrapped around his waist, he went to her kitchen to fix himself a drink, then back to the bedroom. For a long moment, he looked down at the woman in the bed.

The sex between them had always been good but meaningless. And tonight when he'd begun to make love to her, the meaninglessness of it overwhelmed him to the point where he'd had to stop. As he looked at her now, he realized that he felt...nothing. Absolutely nothing.

That was usually enough.

But not tonight.

He crossed the bedroom to the undraped window. Leaning his bare shoulder against the frame, he took a long swallow of his scotch and stared into the night.

He found himself wondering if Kyra was alone at that moment.

Or if she was with a man. For all he knew, she could have been living with someone. After all, she had a child.

Jack restlessly dragged his fingers through his still-damp hair. It was none of his business.

She was nothing to him.

Just an assistant.

Chapter 4

Kyra arrived at work early the next morning before anyone else.

The first thing she did was hang up the dress she'd brought for that evening's dinner party. Reaching over her desk, she turned on her computer to make it look as though she was working at her own area in case anyone came in.

Then she went straight into Jack's office, closed the door and started going through his desk. There were files in the bottom right-hand drawer and she went through each one looking for something—anything—that was out of place. An invoice. A letter. A notation.

But there was nothing incriminating. The only thing she discovered was that he was neat and had an eye for detail.

Next she went through his appointment book. Starting with the first of the year, she examined every day up to the present. There were all kinds of meetings with recognizable Washington bigwigs listed, including a lot of lunches and some dinners with Burton Banacomp. Most of the meetings with Banacomp and the others occurred in Chicago, which meant that they were going after Jack's support rather than the other way around.

She found that interesting but not unusual. Politicians were constantly going where the money was. It was their life's blood.

The problem was figuring out if Banacomp was in league with any of the others. A cursory look told her that when Jack met with the congressman, it was alone or with Barry. Never with another politician.

Kyra took a legal pad out of Jack's middle desk drawer and began scribbling down names for Riley to check out along with the dates and locations of the meetings.

She worked fast, but not fast enough. A look at her watch told her that others would be arriving anytime.

She put everything back in its proper place, then stepped away from the desk to make sure she hadn't overlooked anything.

Perfect.

"What are you doing?"

Kyra's heart slammed against her ribs as she whirled around to find Jack Allessandro standing in the doorway watching her. "Nothing really," she lied as she casually dangled the legal pad from her left hand with the pages turned away from him. "Just seeing if you left any instructions for me. I thought you were going to be gone today."

"I am," he said tersely as he moved past her to his desk. "I just stopped in for a file. And if I had left any instructions for you, I would have put them on your desk, not mine."

"Of course. I was just trying to cover all of the bases." She started to leave his office.

"Ms. Courtland?"

Kyra wanted to get the legal pad out of sight, but she had to turn back. "Yes?"

"How is your taste in jewelry?"

"Do you mean my taste in general or in terms of what I can afford?" She had meant to be amusing, but he didn't smile.

"Your taste in terms of what *I* can afford," he said as he took a file from his middle drawer and dropped it into his briefcase.

"Oh, well, then I'd have to say I have an unerring eye. Almost anyone would."

He snapped his briefcase closed and moved around the desk to stand in front of her. To Kyra's surprise, Jack raised his hand and gently fingered her delicate gold hoop earring. "That's very pretty."

"Thirty-four dollars and ninety-five cents on sale at Sak's." She was uncomfortable being this close to him, but she didn't step away.

"I want you to pick out something for me to give to Barbara—Ms. Wendt."

"Anything in particular?"

"I don't know. Earrings. A bracelet."

"Is there a price limit?"

"Under ten thousand." His hand fell to his side.

"You know," said Kyra quietly, "if I were Barbara, I'd rather have you pick out something for me yourself, even if it's not in perfect taste. A gift has no real meaning otherwise.''

His eyes looked into hers. ''But you're not Barbara, are you?''

His words were almost a challenge.

Then he brushed past her as he walked out the door. ''Have it ready for me tonight.''

''Yes, sir.'' Kyra walked into her own office and angrily slammed the legal pad onto her desk. Buying Jack Allessandro's mistress a gift wasn't in her job description, but she was stuck with it. She couldn't make a fuss without risking her job at this point.

''Kim,'' she said into her speakerphone, ''I have to buy a nice piece of jewelry at Mr. Allessandro's request. Is there a good store nearby?''

''Tiffany's is just a few blocks away.''

''Does he have an account there?''

''I don't know. Just tell them who it's for. If he doesn't have one already, I'm sure they won't have a problem opening one.''

''Thanks.''

Ripping the pages from the legal pad, she folded them and put them in her purse before heading out of the office.

It was a beautiful day, and Kyra had to admit that she liked Chicago. She always had. Downtown, at least, seemed clean and safe. People were dressed up and in a hurry, as in any big city, but that didn't stop them from smiling if they made eye contact, and politely holding doors open for those coming in behind them.

She also liked the architecture. Old and new combined beautifully.

By the time she'd walked the three blocks to Tiffany's, she was relaxed and in a better mood. An elegantly dressed associate approached her with a smile. "May I help you?"

"I hope so. I need to buy a gift for someone I don't know very well."

"Do you have anything special in mind?"

Kyra looked at the display case in front of her and saw a very delicate gold bracelet with emeralds embedded in the clasp. "May I see that?" she asked, pointing it out.

The woman unlocked the case and removed the bracelet. "Would you like to try it on?"

"Yes, thank you."

The woman fastened it onto Kyra's wrist, then turned a mirror toward her so she could see how it looked. "It's beautiful. If I were buying it for myself, this is what I'd get. But somehow I don't think it's quite right for the intended recipient."

The woman unfastened the bracelet and placed it back in the case.

"Just out of curiosity, how much is it?"

"Fifteen thousand dollars."

Just a tad out of her price range, thought Kyra as she moved on to another case and then another. "This is it," said Kyra suddenly, pointing at another gold bracelet, this time a chunkier one made up of Tiffany's signature x's. It was a beautiful piece—simple, but large enough to suit Barbara's height. "It's perfect for her."

"Would you like the earrings to match?"

"Perhaps another time. Just wrap that, if you'd be so kind, and charge it to Jack Allessandro."

"Of course."

Their version of wrapping turned out to be putting it in a blue box and tying it with a white ribbon.

With the box safely tucked away in her shoulder bag, Kyra quickly walked back to the office.

She worked on returning calls and answering E-mail until people began leaving for lunch.

Then she went back into Jack's office. Turning on his computer, she began opening the files that didn't require a password. One of those was a list of names, addresses and telephone numbers.

Kyra hit the print button and waited impatiently while page after page rolled out. She looked at them one at a time and noticed that he had the private office and home number of several politicians. Kyra underlined those to bring them to Riley's attention.

It could mean something, or it could mean nothing.

She returned to her own office to put the papers into her shoulder bag, then went back to Jack's office for what little time she had left before people started returning from lunch.

Quickly viewing the files she could get access to, everything seemed aboveboard. But there were a lot of password-locked files that looked interesting. She would have to save those for another day.

Just as she shut everything down, the door opened and Barry Chesler stood there, as surprised to see Kyra as she was to see him.

"What are you doing in here?" he asked.

Kyra's heart was hammering, but her smile was relaxed. "Working hard."

"Why in here?"

"I was just checking Mr. Allessandro's calendar to make sure I wasn't missing anything on mine."

"Can you do that in your own office? I need to use Jack's computer. Mine's down."

"Of course." She picked up Jack's daybook as she rose from the chair. "Would you like me to call someone to fix your computer?"

"I'll have Kim take care of that. Thanks anyway."

One of the things that Kyra had learned was that since Barry wasn't really active in the business side of the company, he had very little paperwork. He used Kim to answer his calls and type whatever correspondence he had. He wasn't even in the office all that often; perhaps two days a week, and then only for a few hours.

"I understand you're taking care of the dinner this evening," Barry said as he lowered himself into Jack's chair and turned on the computer.

"That's right. Will you be there?"

"Of course. Somebody has to supply the charm." He winked at her.

Kyra smiled at him as she left the office and closed the door behind her.

Two close calls in one day, she thought as she hugged Jack's daybook to her breast. She was going to have to be more careful. Smuggling wasn't child's play. If Jack was involved, Barry probably was, too. And if either of them were to suspect she was other than who she said she was, she could be in big trouble.

Kyra spent the rest of the afternoon sitting at her desk, doing her job. Every once in a while, she would notice the light on her phone go on, indicating that

Barry was using Jack's phone. He was in there for a long time.

When she finally finished the last letter, Kyra looked at her watch. Almost five. She really needed to see about the dinner preparations. "Kim?" she said as she pressed the intercom button to the reception area.

"Yes?"

"Has the caterer arrived?"

"He and his assistant are already working in the kitchen."

"Thanks."

"It's time for me to head home. Is there anything you want me to do before I leave?"

"No, thanks for asking. I'll talk to you in the morning."

Kyra hung up and opened the door to Jack's office.

Barry was gone, apparently through his own connecting door.

Kyra went through the door on the opposite wall that led into a boardroom. The boardroom opened into a lovely receiving area with a bar, which opened into a formal dining room, which in turn opened into a large gourmet kitchen. Kyra pushed open the double doors as she walked from one room to the next, finally entering the kitchen. It was bustling with activity and wonderful aromas.

"Hello," she said as she surveyed the preparations. "I'm Kyra Courtland, Mr. Allessandro's assistant. Thank you for doing this on such short notice. Do you know if the flowers have arrived?"

"I haven't seen them," said the man.

The woman shrugged her shoulders. "I've only been here a few minutes myself."

"I'll look around."

She did. No flowers. So she called the florist to see where they were. The florist claimed they were on their way.

Kyra went to the dining room and started going through the cabinets. She found some beautiful china and silverware that would look splendid on the round, inlaid rosewood table. The crystal was exquisite and the linen napkins were still in their dry-cleaning wrappers. She did one complete place setting then stepped back and studied it.

The napkin wasn't right.

She changed the folds, arranged it on the plate and stepped back to study it again.

Perfect.

One at a time, she worked on the other place settings until the table was ready—except for the flowers, which still hadn't arrived. She found some lovely candles that she set at staggered intervals to complement the size and shape of the table. In the cabinets where the china had been, she found the perfect vase for the floral arrangement she had in mind.

As she was finishing that task, the bartender arrived. He began setting out what he'd brought with him and getting the glasses ready in the reception area.

Returning to the kitchen, she checked on the hors d'oeuvres, then called the florist again. For the second time, she was assured that the flowers would arrive shortly.

Kyra went back to her office and took her dress out

of the closet. She had her own bathroom just off her office so stepped inside to change into the above-the-knee, sleeveless black dress with a high mandarin collar that gently hugged her figure. Leaning against the counter with one hand, she slipped her feet into her high heels then turned to the mirror to check her hair and makeup.

She wasn't exactly a mess, but she definitely needed some work. Taking her hair out of its twist, she brushed it and put it neatly back up. She also freshened her makeup a little then gave herself a critical once-over. She looked professional rather than sexy, particularly with her glasses, but still someone Jack Allessandro wouldn't be ashamed to have hostessing for him.

She reached behind to zip the dress the last four inches, but she couldn't grasp it. This was the first time she'd put on this outfit without a saleswoman's help.

She searched through the bathroom drawers, looking for something she could use to extend her reach. Nothing.

Leaving her bathroom, she went into Jack's office and opened the door to his bathroom, thinking she would find something there.

She did.

All six feet three inches of him.

There stood Jack, bare chested with a towel wrapped low around his waist, his jaw covered in shaving cream and a razor in his hand.

Her eyes huge, Kyra took a step back. "Oh! Excuse me! I...I...I..."

His eyes met hers in the mirror. He looked more curious than annoyed. "What are you doing here?"

"I couldn't get my dress zipped. I was looking for something to catch the tab so I could pull it the rest of the way up. I didn't know you were here."

"Don't get so flustered, Ms. Courtland. Surely you've seen a man without a shirt before."

"Well, yes, but…but…but…" Not one who looked quite like he did, she thought to herself. He was beautifully sculpted, from his shoulders down to his…towel. His very low-riding towel.

She had to force her eyes to his face. "I'll wait for you in your office."

"Just a minute." He wiped the remaining shaving cream from his face with a few swipes of a towel, then walked behind her. Kyra's heart went straight to her throat when his hands touched her back. She felt a gentle pressure as he finished zipping her up.

Her heart was hammering wildly. "Thank you."

"What have you found out about the Greek?" he asked as he walked past her into his office, then went to his closet and pulled out a pair of trousers. "I want to see how accurate your observations were."

Kyra watched as he went back into his bathroom and left the door slightly ajar. She was having trouble focusing her mind, but she gave it a shot. Riley had managed to get a little information to her. "I contacted some of the names he mentioned and, indeed, he's very much a peripheral acquaintance, nothing more. And I also spoke with the last company he sold some of his bargain freighters to, and was told that they've had nothing but trouble with them."

"What kind of trouble?"

"Bad engines and leaking storage tanks."

Jack walked out of his bathroom wearing trousers but still no shirt. "Good job."

"Thank you." She watched as he pulled a shirt off a hanger and put it on. She'd done her best to think of Jack Allessandro as a subject to study. Sometimes she was more successful at it than others, but she tried. At this moment, though, she was very much aware of him as a man and it made her extremely uncomfortable.

"Tonight," he said, turning to her as he buttoned the shirt, "I want you to do your best to make everyone feel at ease. All of the people here are involved in their own companies. I'm interested in doing business with them and it's important that they feel valued."

"I know. You told me that yesterday."

He tucked in his shirt then pulled a tie off of a rack and draped it around his neck. "I'm counting on you."

"I understand." She smoothed her dress with nervous hands. "If you'll excuse me, there are some last-minute things I need to check on." She all but fled his office.

Jack stared after her as he knotted his tie. He didn't quite know what to make of this new assistant of his.

Kyra walked quickly to the reception room. Her heart was pounding. She knew why and she didn't like it. She had investigated other attractive men— even dangerous men. She'd worked with them.

Jack was different, though.

At least, her reaction to him was different.

The bartender turned when she walked into the

room. "The florist delivered a box for you," he said.
"I put it in the dining room."

"Thank you." Kyra found it lying across the arms
of one of the chairs. Tugging on one end of the gold
bow, she untied it and removed the lid. The flowers
were beautiful, long stemmed and ready to arrange,
just as she had asked.

Taking the vase she'd found earlier from the side-
board, she carried the flowers into the kitchen, filled
the vase with water and began snipping the stems to
the right length and skillfully arranging them, just as
she had done so many times for her father's gather-
ings.

Carrying the bouquet into the dining room, she
placed it on the table, then stood back to look at it.

It wasn't quite right.

She rearranged some of the blossoms.

As she was doing that, Jack started to pass by the
open door, but saw Kyra there and stopped to watch.
He was struck by how right she looked standing there
in her simple black dress bent over the flowers and
gracefully arranging them. His eyes moved over her
fine profile. He wondered what she would look like
with her hair down. And without her glasses.

"The table looks very nice," he said in his quiet
voice.

Kyra straightened away from the flowers and studied the table with a critical eye. Then she looked at
him and smiled. "Thank you."

Jack felt his heart catch—a most unfamiliar sensation.

Determined to get a grip on whatever it was this
man made her feel, Kyra met it head on. "Your tie

is crooked,'' she said as she stood in front of him and adjusted the knot, then smoothed her hands over the lapels of his suit jacket.

She hadn't intended it to be an intimate gesture, but it was.

Jack reached up and put his hands over hers.

Chapter 5

Kyra nervously backed away from him. "I bought the gift for Barbara you asked me to. It's a bracelet. I put it in your top right-hand desk drawer. I think she'll really like it."

"What about you? Is it the kind of gift you'd like to receive?"

"Any woman would. And this particular bracelet suits your mis—suits Barbara perfectly."

"But not you?" he guessed.

"I found one I would have preferred for myself, but then I wasn't buying it for me." Kyra looked at her watch. "Would you mind if I made a quick call home to say good-night to my son?"

"Of course not."

"I won't be long."

Kyra walked past Jack on the way to her office, leaving him standing in a soft cloud of her delicate scent.

Sitting behind her desk, she dialed her number. Her aunt answered.

"Hello," said Kyra. "Is Noah still up?"

"We were just reading a story."

"Would you put him on, please? I don't know what time I'll be home tonight."

"Just get here when you can. Everything's fine."

Kyra could hear her talking to Noah. The phone was dropped for a moment, but then Noah's voice came across the line. "Mommy?"

"Hi, sweetheart. I understand Aunt Emily is reading you a story."

"Goo'night Moon."

"I'll be home late tonight, after you're already asleep. But I'll come see you as soon as I get there. And tomorrow night I'll read to you."

"'Kay."

"I love you, Noah."

"'Kay."

"Bye. Sweet dreams."

"Bye."

The door of her office opened. "They're arriving," Jack said.

Kyra followed him through his office and back to the reception room where there was a special elevator, elegantly disguised with elaborately carved doors that were works of art in their own right. Barry stepped off the elevator with the guests. He'd clearly been entertaining them up to now.

Barry took one look at Kyra and raised an eyebrow. She looked inquiringly back, wondering if she'd blundered with her dress. Then he gave her a discreet thumbs-up.

Jack introduced her formally as Ms. Courtland to the guests as they came off the elevator. He made sure her position as his assistant was very clear.

The last man who got off the elevator had brought his young—very young—wife. It was unexpected and obvious to Kyra that the woman knew a mistake had been made almost as soon as she arrived.

As the bartender was getting everyone a drink, the woman came up to Kyra and touched her arm. "I'm so sorry," she said in labored English. "We thought this was for…" She searched for the word.

Kyra smiled kindly. "Couples," she said in Spanish. "Please don't apologize, Mrs. Sanchez," she said, also in Spanish. "Mr. Allessandro, Mr. Chesler and I are all happy to have you here. I only wish the others had thought to bring their wives, as well. I think women in a group make for a much more pleasant evening, don't you?"

She still seemed worried. "If I had met them for cocktails before, I would have known. But my husband told me to meet him downstairs. You're sure it isn't a problem?"

"I'm sure." Even though Kyra was dying to know what Jack was talking to the others about, she stayed with the insecure woman to make her feel more at ease.

But she did manage to watch both Jack and Barry at work. There was a clear division of labor. Barry was witty and charming, telling jokes.

Jack was talking business. She could tell from his demeanor. The men would tire of laughing with Barry and wander over to Jack. Or they would tire of talking business and wander over to Barry.

Kyra, with her arm looped through that of Mrs. Sanchez, went from person to person to see if anyone needed anything and to make small talk. When she could manage it without looking as though she was dumping the woman, she returned her to her husband.

Kyra was unaware of it, but Jack's eyes followed her around the room. For the first time in his adult life, he was having trouble focusing on business because of a woman.

And Barry noticed.

Kyra, without Mrs. Sanchez, approached two men who were standing alone and talking. "May I get either of you anything?" she asked.

One of the men put his arm around her waist, pulled her to his side and waved his drink at the other one. "You can settle a bet."

"About what?" Kyra reached up and unfastened her earring, just as her mother had taught her to do as a teenager when situations like this arose.

Jack excused himself from the man he was with and crossed the room to Kyra. Taking her by the wrist, he inclined his head toward the man who had his arm around her. "If you'll excuse the interruption, I need to speak with my assistant."

"Of course, of course." The man winked broadly as his hand fell to his side. "If I had an assistant like this one, I'd need to talk to her, as well. And often."

Kyra could feel Jack's anger in the way his grip tightened on her, but it didn't show in his demeanor or voice. "If you had an assistant like Ms. Courtland," he said quietly but firmly, "you'd have to have your 'talks' with someone else."

The man knew he'd been very politely told that

Kyra wasn't that kind of woman. He acknowledged it by raising his glass to Jack. "My apologies," he said.

Jack inclined his head, but said nothing.

Then he literally pulled Kyra into the dining room and slid the doors closed. "What do you think you're doing?" he asked, anger in every syllable.

"What?" she asked, truly bewildered.

"This is a business dinner. You're here in a professional capacity, not to throw yourself at the guests."

Kyra's lips parted in astonishment. "Throw myself—?"

"Do it again and you're fired." He started to open the doors to return to the guests, but Kyra grabbed his arm.

"I'll have you know," she said as quietly as her anger would allow, "that I have never thrown myself at anyone at any time in my life. If you had simply stayed where you were, everything would have been fine." She opened her palm and showed him the earring. "I was about to drop this and bend to pick it up. In two seconds, I would have been too far away for him to touch. He wouldn't have known what happened, much less have been embarrassed by it."

Jack's eyes were locked with hers. "Just do your job, Ms. Courtland." Jack opened the doors and left, sliding them closed behind him and leaving Kyra fuming in the dining room.

She stood still for several seconds, just breathing deeply, her fists clenched so hard the earring dug into her palm.

"Ms. Courtland?" a voice said from behind her.

She turned to find the chef standing there.

"The first course is ready to serve."

She waited a moment before answering, deliberately calming herself. "Thank you. I'll get everyone seated."

She pushed Jack from her mind as she quickly set an extra place for Mrs. Sanchez, rearranged the others, then slid open the doors. Rather than approaching Jack, she went to Barry. "Dinner is ready whenever we can get people seated."

Barry signaled Jack and the two of them began herding people toward the dining room.

Kyra seated Mrs. Sanchez beside her. It wasn't her first choice, but it was really the only polite thing to do.

Throughout dinner, she managed to avoid looking at Jack. She did, however, manage to keep one ear on his conversation.

Jack, it seemed, was trying to talk all of these people into using his freighters. But he said nothing that was unexpected or that even remotely suggested there was anything illegal going on.

Not that she expected him to come right out in the open with it, but she was ever hopeful that he would make her job easier.

Just then, Mrs. Sanchez reached for her wine and accidentally knocked it over. She looked as though she wanted to die right there. And her husband didn't look any too happy with her.

Kyra quickly threw her napkin over the spill. "I'm so sorry," she said as though she was the one who had done it. "I'm not usually so clumsy. I'll have that cleaned up in just a minute. I hope nothing got on your lovely dress.''

The woman smiled gratefully at her. ''It's fine, thank you.''

Kyra excused herself to go to the kitchen for a towel to clean up the mess. When she came back, she dabbed up what was left, took her napkin and towel to the kitchen and checked on dessert.

Jack watched Kyra when she returned to the table. His eyes moved over her face feature by feature. She smiled at something someone said and his heart caught, just as it had when she was arranging the flowers.

Kyra looked away from the man she was talking to and straight into Jack's eyes. Her smile slowly faded, but she couldn't look away. There was something in his expression....

The woman beside Kyra touched her arm. She dragged her eyes from Jack's and forced herself to listen. And while she managed, for the most part, to respond appropriately, her thoughts were with the man across from her.

It was ridiculous.

Kyra didn't think the evening would ever end. She smiled and chatted and charmed her way through it, but she was running on automatic pilot. All she wanted to do was go home and get away from Jack Allessandro.

It was nearly one in the morning when she and Jack and Barry finally walked their guests to the elevator. Barry went down with them while Jack stayed with her.

When the door closed, Kyra stood awkwardly in

front of the elevator with Jack. "I left my purse and clothes in my office. I'll just get them and leave."

"I'll have a driver take you home."

"No, thank you. I have my car."

"He'll pick you up in the morning and bring you to work, or I'll have your car delivered. I don't want you driving all the way home alone at this time of night."

"Really, I'd rather go on my own. Besides, you'd probably have to wake someone to take me. There's no point in doing that."

"Don't argue with me. Just give me your keys." His tone and the way he looked at her told her it would be pointless to press the car issue any further. "Get your things. I'll take you myself."

Kyra gave up. She went to her office to collect her clothes and her oversize purse with the information she'd gathered earlier in it and met him in the foyer. Together they took the elevator to the underground parking garage and walked to his black Lexus.

She thought about watching him the night before take this same walk with Barbara.

Jack opened the door for her. As she stepped around him to get into the car, her body brushed against his.

Startled, she glanced at him.

Jack looked wordlessly back at her. He didn't need to say anything. They were both aware of their own intense reactions.

Still in silence, he rounded the car and climbed behind the wheel, then backed the car out of the space and wound his way through the garage until they were traveling on the well lit but deserted Chicago streets.

"You'll have to give me directions," he said.

"Turn left at the next stoplight."

Kyra tried to relax in her seat and not think about the man beside her.

But it was hard.

Her eyes kept moving to his hands.

"I'm sorry about what I said to you earlier this evening," Jack said. "I was concerned about propriety. Some of the people I do business with can be on the rough side—like the man who had his arm around you. I thought you were encouraging yourself into a bad situation."

"I accept your apology but there's really no need for you to concern yourself about me in that way. Believe me when I tell you that I can handle myself. I've been doing it for years without any help."

"I guess you have."

Silence.

"This is a personal question," he said after a few seconds. "If you don't want to answer it, don't. I know you have a child. I'm curious about the baby's father. Is he involved with his child at all?"

Kyra was reluctant to talk about her family with this man. He was the enemy, after all. "He's dead," she said abruptly.

"I'm sorry."

Kyra sighed. She couldn't leave it at that. "Noah's mother was my older sister. She and her husband were killed in—" she had to think for a moment "—an automobile accident when Noah was just a few months old. I adopted him."

It was a terrible thing that had happened, but for

some reason Jack couldn't begin to explain, relief surged through him.

"Turn right here and go straight for the next five miles," Kyra said, interrupting his thoughts.

They both fell silent again as the miles slipped away beneath the tires. Both silent; both aware.

"Have you ever been married?" she asked, knowing the answer but wanting to hear it from him.

"No."

"Why not?"

"When I was younger, I was too busy raising my sister and making my way in the world."

"And now?"

"I think I've grown too selective."

"What about Barbara?"

"That would be between Barbara and me."

"Of course. I'm sorry."

Jack instantly regretted his tone. "I didn't mean it to come out that way."

"It's all right," said Kyra. "I was prying into things that are none of my business."

"So was I, but you didn't bark at me."

Kyra smiled. "The one thing you'll learn about me as we work together is that I'm nothing if not well mannered. My parents wouldn't have it any other way."

"Then I'll presume on your good manners to ask why you're not married."

"I don't really know," she said with a shrug. "I think it's because I'm unwilling to settle for anything less than my ideal."

"You'd rather be alone?" he asked.

"There's nothing wrong with being alone. I'm quite content with my life."

"Is mere contentment enough for you?"

"It has to be, hasn't it?" she said as she turned her head and looked at Jack's profile. "We all have to play the hands we've been dealt. Turn left at the next street."

When Jack pulled up in front of her little house, he got out of the driver's side and walked around to open the door for her.

Kyra put her hand in his so he could help her out. When she was standing on the sidewalk, he didn't release her right away.

They both looked at their clasped hands for a long moment.

Then Kyra gently removed hers. Her heart was pounding. "I appreciate the ride. And the apology. Something tells me you don't apologize very often."

"I don't."

"That makes it doubly appreciated."

"Come in late tomorrow if you want."

"Thank you." Kyra suddenly felt awkward standing there. "Would you like to come in for coffee?"

His eyes looked into hers. The truth was, he would have liked that very much.

Too much.

"No. Good night, Kyra," he said, using her given name for the first time. "And thank you for doing such a nice job on the dinner. It was a good evening, and I know the guests enjoyed it."

"I liked doing it." A smile touched her lips.

Jack studied the dimple that charmingly appeared in her right cheek. He hadn't noticed it before.

"Well," she said, "good night, then. I'll see you tomorrow."

"Wait. I need your keys for the driver."

"Sorry, I forgot." She rummaged around in her purse until she came up with them and dropped them into his outstretched hand. "Thanks."

His gaze followed her into the house.

Kyra closed the door behind her. In darkness, she went to the window and looked outside.

Jack stayed where he was for several minutes, leaning against the front of his car, his arms folded across his chest, watching the house.

Then he straightened and walked around to the driver's side.

Kyra watched as he started the engine. The headlights came on and he backed out of her driveway and disappeared into the distance.

Kyra rested her warm forehead against the cool pane of glass and sighed.

Jack Allessandro could be a crook. An arms smuggler. She shouldn't have to remind herself of that. This was a job. He was the bad guy. There was no place for any kind of emotion.

And yet...

Kyra pushed him from her mind and went to Noah's room. Standing in the doorway, she listened for the comforting sound of his baby breaths before she made her way to his crib. With a gentle hand, she rubbed his back and gazed at him in the soft glow of the blue night-light.

She loved everything about him: The way he

smelled, the way he wrapped his little hand around her finger when they walked, the way he hugged her neck, the way he smiled with those perfect little teeth, the way his eyes lit up when she walked into the room.

Noah filled something in her she hadn't even realized was empty. She couldn't have loved him more if she'd given birth to him.

Leaning over him, she rested her cheek against his, then gently kissed him.

When she got to her own room, Kyra would have methodically followed her evening routine of changing into her T-shirt and boxers, cleaning her face and brushing her teeth—but she couldn't get out of the dress.

Hating to have to do it, she went to her aunt's room and gently woke her. "I'm sorry," she said when her aunt sat up. "I can't get out of my dress."

"Turn around," said Emily.

Kyra did, and sat on the edge of the bed while her aunt found the zipper tab and pulled it down. "How was your evening?" asked the older woman.

"Interesting," Kyra answered vaguely as she rose.

"In what way?"

"Jack Allessandro isn't what I expected."

"Do you want to talk about it?"

Kyra smiled at her aunt as she leaned over and kissed her cheek. "No, but thanks for asking. Sorry I woke you."

"It's all right, dear. Good night."

"Night."

When Kyra got back to her own room, she finished her routine, then climbed beneath the covers of her comfortable but very empty bed, picked a book up from her end table and started to read.

But she couldn't focus her thoughts on the story.

Jack Allessandro kept interrupting.

She could tell herself all she wanted that he was bad news. But there was something about the man that set him apart from other men she'd investigated; set him apart from men she'd dated.

Why was she so attracted to him?

And make no mistake—she was attracted.

Kyra set the book back on the table and turned out the light. Turning onto her side, she slipped one hand under her cheek but didn't close her eyes.

Was this what it felt like to fall in love?

What an odd thought.

It certainly wasn't possible for her to fall in love with a man like Jack Allessandro.

She wouldn't allow herself.

Jack looked at the clock on his dashboard. It was nearly 2:00 a.m. Patty would still be on duty.

He drove through the quiet streets to the hospital, parked in the lot and walked through the sliding doors of the emergency care center.

Patty was standing right there, holding a cup of coffee while she spoke to another doctor. "Jack!" she said in surprise when she saw him. "What on earth are you doing here?"

"I was hoping to catch you on a break."

"Your timing is perfect." She looped her arm through his. "Let's go into the lounge."

The doctors' lounge had a ratty turquoise vinyl-and-metal furniture decor. Patty pushed her brother into a chair and went to the counter to pour him a cup of coffee.

"So what's going on?" she asked as she handed him the plastic cup and sat down across from him.

"What makes you think something's going on?"

Patty raised an expressive brow. "You mean besides the fact that it's nearly three in the morning, you're dressed in a suit and you've never been here before?"

Jack couldn't help smiling.

Patty reached out and touched his cheek. "What is it, big brother?"

"You know people."

"I'd better, or I'm in the wrong business."

"Something happened tonight...." His voice trailed off as he collected his thoughts. "A woman I met a few days ago has a child. I thought it was the product of a relationship she'd had in the past."

"But it wasn't?"

"No. I found out tonight that the child is in fact adopted."

Patty waited for more. When it didn't come, she prodded, "And..."

Jack looked at his sister. "Patty, I can't even describe to you how relieved I was. I mean, I barely know this woman. Her personal life is certainly none of my business. Whether or not she has a child by another man has nothing to do with me."

"I'm not following you," said Patty. "She still has the child."

"Yes."

"So nothing has really changed except that the child is adopted."

"That's right."

As Patty looked at her brother, a slow smile broke across her face.

"What?" asked Jack.

"You don't even know what's going on, do you?" she asked.

"Apparently not. That's why I'm here at this ungodly hour to talk to you."

She leaned forward and touched his hand. "Jack, the simple fact is that you were relieved because you didn't want her to have had a child with another man."

"That's ridiculous."

"It's perfectly normal for a man to want to be the only man to share the experience of childbirth with the woman he loves."

"Love?" Jack looked genuinely shocked. "I barely know her."

"Apparently you know her well enough to have fallen in love."

"That's not possible." He stated it as a fact.

"Why not?"

"Because that would be impulsive, and I'm not an impulsive man."

"That you're a man at all is enough. Don't you know that? Just because you've never fallen in love before doesn't mean that you're incapable of doing it."

"Perhaps I'm just attracted to her."

"Have you ever felt this way about any other woman you've been attracted to?"

Jack didn't have to think about it. "No," he said quietly.

Patty leaned back in her chair and looked at him over the rim of her cup. "Is she in love with you?"

"At this point, I don't think she even likes me very much."

"Well, you can be an SOB at times."

"I know."

"What are you going to do about it?"

"Nothing. I'm not in a position to do anything. And even if I were, I'm not sure I would. It's just a feeling. It will pass."

"If you're in love with her, Jack, trust me when I tell you that it won't pass. Not now. Not ever."

"Perhaps not for a woman. But it's different for a man."

"You think so?"

"Yes," he said with complete sincerity. "Completely. There isn't a woman in the world that I can't live without." He smiled at his sister. "Present company excepted."

"Then you're either very lucky or very sad. I don't know which."

"Lucky." Jack rose, leaned over his sister and kissed her on the cheek. "Thanks for talking to me."

"Any time."

Patty smiled thoughtfully as she watched her brother leave. Men could be so blind when it came to their feelings. She could tell just by looking at Jack that something had affected him profoundly. Apparently it was a woman.

And if he thought he was going to control things, he was very, very mistaken.

She wondered who the woman was who had captured the heart of the man who, up to this point in his life, had remained steadfastly uncatchable.

Chapter 6

Kyra set her alarm an hour later than usual and slept soundly—until she heard Noah making noises like a truck.

She opened her eyes, rolled onto her side and saw him on the floor, crawling behind a red Tonka truck as he pushed it along the rug. She rolled out of bed, picked him up and swung him around. "Good morning, sweetheart."

"Morning!"

She hugged him. "Have you had breakfast yet?"

He shook his head.

"Good. I'll just wash my face and we can eat together." Setting him back on the rug, she walked around him into the bathroom where she washed her face, ran a brush over her teeth and slipped into a robe.

She found Noah already in his booster seat at the

table in the kitchen nook, a spoon clutched in his fist, eating cereal.

Kyra ruffled his hair and sat at the place her aunt had set for her. "It's so nice to have some extra time in the morning," she said as she lifted a glass of juice.

Her aunt set a plate of poached eggs on English muffins in front of her. "You got home late."

"I know. Jack Allessandro drove me."

"Then how did your car get here?"

"My car?" Kyra peered through the kitchen window at her driveway. Sure enough, there was her Jeep. "He must have had it delivered this morning."

Her aunt sat down with her own plate and began putting jam on a triangle of toast. "That was thoughtful."

"Yes, it was," said Kyra quietly.

"And unusual. I don't think most bosses would go to that kind of trouble for a new employee."

Kyra didn't say anything.

"So how did the dinner party go last night?"

"Really well. I was a little nervous at first, but everything fell into place." She changed the subject. "These are really good eggs. Thank you."

"It's good to see you eating for a change. You need to develop better breakfast habits."

"What I need to do is get up earlier, and then breakfast wouldn't be a problem." Kyra aimed her knife at her aunt's toast. "Are you going to eat all of that?"

She pushed her plate closer to Kyra. "Help yourself."

Kyra took one triangle, put a little jam on it and handed it to Noah, who grasped it in his fist and took a big bite right out of the middle. Kyra looked at her aunt and laughed.

"It must be nice to be able to eat with such enthusiastic abandon," said Emily, still smiling.

"That's the way he does everything. It's a wonder to watch." Kyra squinted in the direction of the microwave clock but couldn't make out the numbers without her glasses. "What time is it?"

"A little before ten."

Kyra took a final bite of her eggs, a sip of juice and then wiped her mouth. "I have to go. Jack said I could be late, but I don't think he intended for me to take the day off. I should get dressed."

Her aunt rose also, picking up both plates and carrying them to the sink. "What time will you be home tonight?"

"Six-thirty probably. If there's a change, I'll call you." She kissed the top of Noah's silky head and headed for her room, then abruptly stopped and turned back. "I have an express package that I'm sending to Riley." She'd decided it was too much to fax. "I was told it would be picked up around ten. Will you be here?"

"Sure. I'll see that it gets out."

"Thanks."

Kyra hit the shower and gave herself time to enjoy it. It took only a short time to blow-dry her hair and put on her makeup. She dressed in a navy blue suit that fit her figure well and headed for work.

When she got to the office a short while later, Kyra paused in front of Kim who was at her desk in the reception area. "Is Mr. Allessandro in?"

"In and out," said Kim. "He left a few minutes ago, but he told me he wouldn't be gone long."

"Okay. I guess I'd better get to work. The day's already half-gone."

Kim handed her a stack of messages. "I tried to arrange them in order of importance. You also have several E-mails you need to look at."

"Thanks." Kyra went into her office, put her purse in the small closet, turned on her computer and sat at her desk while she went through her messages. She was growing more familiar with the way things worked. She was still having a little trouble attaching names to faces, but that would come in time.

The door from the reception area opened and a young woman walked into her office. "Excuse me," she said with a charming smile.

Kyra returned the smile. She knew from the Department of Justice file that the woman before her was Jack's younger sister. "Hello. What can I do for you?"

"I came to see Jack, but I understand he's out."

"Yes, but he shouldn't be gone long. Would you like to wait in his office?"

"Sure. Thank you." But she didn't go into Jack's office. Instead, she stayed with Kyra. "I'm Patty Allessandro Phillips," the woman said as she extended her hand. "Jack's sister."

"Kyra Courtland," she said, returning the courtesy. "Your brother's new assistant."

"How are you liking your job here?"

"Very much. I haven't been at it long, but I'm starting to get the hang of things."

"I think I remember Eleanor telling me that you came here from Virginia."

"That's right."

"I imagine it's quite an adjustment."

"I live in a suburb, so things aren't all that different. I guess I'm a little isolated at the moment because I haven't had time to really meet anyone. Not even my new neighbors."

"Meeting people is one of the hardest things about relocating. More so for adults than children, I think."

"I know. My son seems to be adjusting just fine."

Patty's ears perked up. Son? She looked at Kyra with a sudden smile. "Listen, my husband and I are having a cookout tomorrow. There will be a lot of people there. Why don't you come? And bring your husband and child."

"I'm not married. I live with an aunt."

Patty smiled a little wider. "Then bring her along."

"That's very kind. But are you sure your brother won't be upset with you?"

"Why would he be?"

"Because I work for him. It might be awkward."

"Don't worry about Jack. It's my party and I want you to come."

This was a wonderful stroke of luck for Kyra. If she could become friends with Patty, it would mean better access to others in the family, and might even increase her access to Jack. "Thank you. We'll be there."

"How old is your child?"

"Two."

"Perfect. He's almost the same age as my daughter. This is going to be fun."

She ripped a blank sheet of paper out of Kyra's notebook, picked up a pen and scribbled her address and home telephone number on it. "We're really easy to find, but if you get lost, just call that number and we'll guide you in."

Jack walked in to find his sister perched on the edge of Kyra's desk. "What are you doing here, Patty?"

She stood up. "I have an hour before I'm back on duty. I thought maybe we could grab lunch together."

Jack looked at his watch. "Sure." Then he looked at Kyra and his expression changed in a way Patty couldn't define. It was subtle. "Did you get some sleep?"

"Yes. Thank you for letting me come in late. I also appreciate your having my car delivered."

Patty looked at her brother with interest. He was never this solicitous of people.

"Your consideration of Mrs. Sanchez last night at dinner has already paid dividends. Her husband called this morning. He's going to be using our freighters for at least the next year."

"I'm glad."

"I'll be with you in a minute, Patty." He went into his office and came out with a file. He leaned over Kyra's shoulder as he opened the file and pointed out a letter.

God, he smelled good, Kyra thought.

"This is from our Greek friend. Write back and tell him we aren't interested, but be diplomatic. Have it ready when I get back from lunch. I want it to go out as soon as I've signed it."

Without waiting for a response, Jack left with his sister.

Kyra sat staring at the closed door. What was it about that man that affected her so? She almost resented him for making her feel the way she did. It wasn't right. It was unprofessional.

It was his fault.

With a shake of her head, she turned back to her computer. The sooner she could get the information she needed, the sooner she could get out of here and back to Virginia.

Patty sat across from Jack at the small restaurant table and chewed on a bread stick while she looked at her brother.

"What?" asked Jack, sounding irritated. "You've been staring at me since we left the office."

Patty smiled. "I can't help myself. I'm not used to seeing you like this."

"Like what?"

"Soft and fuzzy around the hard edges."

"What are you talking about?"

"Ms. Kyra Courtland."

"What about her?"

"I have never in my life seen you look at a woman the way you looked at her this afternoon."

Jack was genuinely mystified. "What way?"

"You like her, Jack. You more than like her."

"For heaven's sake, Patty, how old are you? Ten?"

She grinned at him. "I know what I saw."

"Your imagination is running away with you. I barely know the woman."

"Like you barely know the woman you were telling me about last night. The unmarried one with a child.''

Jack leaned back in his chair, clearly irritated. ''Look, I needed someone to talk to last night. Don't start throwing my words back at me or you can bet I won't make that mistake again.''

''You're right.'' Patty rubbed his hand. ''I'm sorry. I just couldn't help but put two and two together.''

''Your addition is off.''

''No, it's not. I don't think even you're aware of what's going on.''

''And you are? After what? Five minutes?''

''Less.''

''Yeah, well, I appreciate your keen insights, but don't quit your day job, Doctor.''

Patty smiled as she bit off another chunk of her bread stick.

''Don't start, Patty,'' he warned.

Kyra finished the letter along with some other work Jack had left for her and checked her watch. He would probably be back anytime, so she didn't want to risk getting caught going through his files again. That would be for another day.

Instead, she began moving around inside her own computer to see what kinds of things she had access to that might help in the investigation. What she found—and didn't like at all—was that when she went from department to department, she had to log in separately each time with her own log-in number.

That meant that if anyone was interested, they could see where she'd been and what she'd been looking at. No one had any reason to be suspicious of her, but if someone decided to get a little curious, it could be very telling.

The alternative was to figure out how to access the information with someone else's log-in number so she could cover her tracks. That shouldn't be too hard.

For now, since she was in the system anyway, she printed out a shipping schedule that included particular freighters that belonged to Allessandro Shipping, what they would be carrying, the weight, the value, the estimated cost of transport as well as destinations, travel dates and companies involved.

More telling than any of it was the scheduled purchase and shipping of government scrap. Lots of companies did that. It wasn't illegal. In fact, the government encouraged it with huge auctions.

But what if some of the scrap was classified?

And what if Jack knew it?

He would definitely be going to prison for a long, long time.

Kyra didn't have time to check the entire shipping schedule for cargos headed for China or Iran specifically, so she hit the print button and waited.

Just as the document finished coming out of the printer, she heard Jack's voice in the reception area. She quickly shut off her computer screen because she hadn't had time to key out, grabbed the sheet of paper and was placing it under a file when he walked into her office.

"Did you have a nice lunch?" she asked.

He looked at her but didn't answer right away.

In fact, he was silent for so long that she was afraid she'd somehow given herself away.

"It was lunch. Nothing special," he finally said.

But there was something odd in his tone. "Is everything all right?"

Jack's eyes moved over her face as though searching for something.

"Yes, I suppose it is," he said absently. Then he seemed to shake off whatever was bothering him. "Any messages?"

"Yes, several."

"Bring them to me along with the letter," he said as he walked into his office.

Kyra picked up what he'd asked for along with the other letters and followed after him. As she sat down, he removed his jacket and loosened his tie.

As soon as he was seated, Jack began going through his messages, then through his mail and told her what to do with it letter by letter. The interesting thing was that he didn't dictate responses so much as give her a sense of what she should write. Kyra rather liked that. It certainly meant he trusted her ability.

They were finished with the entire stack within an hour. But Kyra knew she had at least three hours of typing ahead of her. "Would you like me to stay late to finish these?" she asked.

"Just do the ones that require an immediate response. Leave the others until Monday."

"All right. And what about the response to Mr. Zukos?"

Jack went over it very carefully. "Well done," he said without looking at her as he signed it. "See that it gets out tonight."

"Anything else?"

"No," he said without looking up.

She was definitely dismissed.

Kyra worked hard and fast. Everything was finished by six o'clock. Stacking her work, she carried it into Jack's office. "They just need your signature," she said as she set them in front of him.

She watched him as he read through the letters and signed them.

"You're very good," he said as he handed them back to her. "You catch on quickly."

"Thank you."

His eyes met hers. "I'm going to Spain on Monday. I need you to come with me. Is that a problem?"

"Not at all."

"Good. I'll have a car pick you up at your home at 7 a.m. for the ride to the airport."

"I'll be ready. Will I need any formal clothes?"

"Yes. Evening is a prime time to conduct business there."

"And how long will we be gone?"

"Three days. The Sanchezes will be there. They're both looking forward to seeing you again."

"I'll be extra charming," she said as she picked up the mail and returned to her own office.

Spain, she thought. With Jack Allessandro.

It was a job.

No problem.

She was at her desk folding the letters and putting them in envelopes when Jack's girlfriend walked in.

Once again, Barbara completely ignored Kyra. And Kyra gave Barbara Wendt the same courtesy.

When the last of the letters were in their envelopes and ready to be mailed, Kyra tidied her desk, pushed in her chair and went to her closet for her purse.

As she closed the closet door, she looked up and into the eyes of Jack Allessandro.

Kyra met his gaze for just a moment, then looked away.

It was time to go home.

She dropped the letters in a lobby mailbox, then went directly to her car and drove home. When she arrived, her aunt was alone in the living room working on a crossword puzzle, her reading glasses on the end of her nose. "Hello, dear," she said with a smile.

Kyra bent to kiss her cheek. "Where's Noah?"

"Already sound asleep. He was so tired after play group that it was all I could do to keep him awake long enough to eat dinner and take a bath. I kept a plate warm in the oven for you."

"Thanks, Aunt Emily," said Kyra as she headed for the kitchen.

"There's a FedEx package for you on the counter."

Kyra picked it up and ripped the tab to open it. The password-finder disk was inside. She set it on the counter and tossed the envelope in the trash.

Taking her plate out of the oven, she set some silverware on it, picked up her purse and the disk, then walked back through the living room. "I have some work to do, Aunt Emily. If it's all right with you, I'll just eat in my room."

"Of course it's all right."

"Oh!" Kyra said as she walked back into the living room. "I accepted an invitation to a cookout tomorrow afternoon. You and Noah are included. I hope that's all right with you."

"Sounds like fun. Who's hosting?"

"Jack Allessandro's younger sister, Patty, and her husband."

"Is your boss going to be there?"

"Probably."

"Then I'm doubly looking forward to it. I want to meet the mysterious Jack Allessandro."

"Aunt Emily..."

The older woman smiled gently at her niece. "Do you honestly think you can hide from me the fact that something is going on between the two of you?"

"There is not." Kyra's denial was earnest but unconvincing.

"Dear, I know that whatever it is you're doing, you'll do best if you're trusted and get as close as possible to those you're investigating. It's perfectly logical. But don't let yourself get in so deep that you lose sight of the reason for the relationship in the first place."

Kyra set her plate on the coffee table and sank onto the couch. "Jack's different," said Kyra. "I've never met anyone like him."

"Do you think Riley is right about him?"

Kyra smiled. "You always know more than I think you do." Her smile faded. "I don't know. My reaction to him is so visceral that I can't see clearly what kind of man he is. I know I'm more attracted to him than I've ever been to any other man."

"Why?"

"I don't know," Kyra said, shaking her head. "And, believe me, I've tried to analyze it because I know I need to move past whatever it is I'm feeling. It makes it difficult to do my job."

"Particularly when your job is to betray his trust."

Kyra looked down at her hands.

"Have you thought about calling Riley and asking him to take you off this case?"

"Not seriously. I'm really the only one he could send in. And if Jack is guilty, he's responsible not just for the smuggling of what could be national secrets and high-tech weapons, but the deaths of the people murdered with them and the threat to safety and peace in our own country. I can't let that go."

"Then you'll do what you have to in order to discover the truth."

Kyra rubbed her aching forehead. "You know, I've been assigned to cases where I did everything I could to get close to the people I was investigating. With this one, where a friendship or even the hint of a romance that never comes to fruition could be so beneficial, I'm doing everything I can to avoid it."

"Why do you think that is?"

She looked at her aunt. "Because all the other times, I was the one who was in control. I decided how far to take things and where to draw the line. With Jack, I'm afraid I won't know where that line is. Or, if I do see it, I'll be too out of control to stop. You have no idea how much that thought frightens me."

"No, but I can imagine."

Kyra rubbed her forehead and sighed softly. "I'm so tired, I could sleep for a week."

"Go to bed early tonight."

Kyra nodded as she rose. "Thanks for listening," she said as she kissed her aunt's cheek. "I'm going to finish my work and take your advice about going to bed early. Good night."

She picked up her plate and went to her room.

Sitting down at her computer, she connected with Riley's and typed in the information she thought was pertinent, then faxed the rest to him using her scanner.

When she was finished, Kyra sank tiredly onto her bed, ignoring her dinner completely, and fell sound asleep on top of her covers, still in her clothes.

There were no dreams. No nightmares.

Just a deep, exhausted sleep.

Chapter 7

Kyra set Noah's sneakers in front of him on the floor, the right one in front of the right foot and the left one in front of the left foot.

It was a matter of great pride to him that he could put on his own shoes.

But it also took him a long time.

Kyra waited patiently until he was finished, then helped him tighten the Velcro straps. "Ready to go?" she asked as she fastened the snap on the bib of his overalls.

He nodded. "Weddy."

Aunt Emily walked in and ruffled his blond hair. "Come on. We're going to be late. Your car or mine, Kyra?"

"Mine's already in the driveway." She looked admiringly at her aunt's flowing skirt. "You look nice."

"I'm too old to wear jeans to cookouts."

"Not with a figure like yours, you're not. But I like the skirt."

"Thanks, dear. I haven't been out for a while so I'm actually looking forward to this."

Kyra gave Noah a little pat on the bottom. "Let's go, big fella."

It was a gorgeous day. Kevin and Patty's home was only thirty minutes away, right on the shore of Lake Michigan. Kyra found it more easily than she expected.

It was a striking home, large and made of red brick with canopies over the windows and a winding brick sidewalk leading to the front double doors. Kyra parked the Jeep behind a long line of cars on the street.

"It looks like a big cookout," said Aunt Emily.

Kyra sighed as she looked out the windshield.

"What's wrong, dear?"

What *was* wrong? This was work for her. She had to watch, listen and manage to look as though she was enjoying herself. "Nothing," she said with a smile. "Nothing at all."

She stepped out of the car, unfastened Noah from his car seat and stood back while he turned around and climbed out backward.

They could hear voices and laughter as they approached the house. Rather than knocking on the front door, they walked around the side. Patty was standing a few feet away facing them.

She smiled and quickly walked toward them. "Kyra, I'm glad you came."

"This is my aunt, Emily Mason, and my son, Noah."

Patty shook Emily's hand, then kneeled in front of Noah and shook his hand, too. "It's nice to meet you, Noah."

He didn't say anything.

"How old are you?"

Still the child said nothing, but he raised his hand and put up two fingers.

"Two!" said Patty with a wide smile. "You're nearly grown. I bet you'll like my little girl. Her name is Mandy. Would you like to come with me and find her?"

Noah wrapped his arm around Kyra's leg and looked shyly up at Patty through his long lashes.

"I'm sorry," said Kyra as she stroked his hair. "He likes to check people out for a while before he carries on a conversation."

"He's a wise child," said Patty as she straightened and signaled to a man a few yards away to come to her. He approached them with a friendly smile and put his arm around Patty's shoulders. "Kyra Courtland and Emily Mason, I'd like to introduce you to my husband, Kevin. Kyra is Jack's new assistant, the one I told you about." Patty's tone was full of meaning. "Noah is her little boy and Emily is her aunt."

Kevin gave Kyra's hand a vigorous shake and then Emily's. "It's so nice to meet you both. And you, too, Noah. I'm glad you could come."

"You have a lovely home here," said Emily. "And your view is nothing short of splendid."

Kevin turned to look at the lake. "It's an interesting body of water," agreed Kevin. "Lake Michigan is very much a force to be dealt with. Sometimes when there's a storm, the lake gets so loud and violent that you can scream in the ear of the person you're standing beside and they still can't hear you.''

"I think I'd like that," said Emily.

Patty was eyeing Kyra. She liked her. She had from the first moment they'd met. And she was perfect for Jack. Patty had a nose for these things, whether the men in her life wanted to admit it or not.

"Noah," said Patty as she leaned over the little boy, "would you like to play with the other children?"

He looked up at Kyra.

"Would you like to do that?" asked Kyra.

He nodded.

"Then come with me," said Patty as she took his hand. "I'll take you to them." She looked at Kyra. "You don't have to worry about him. He'll be carefully watched by the older children. We've done this before and they're very trustworthy."

"Thank you."

Emily touched her niece's arm. "I'm going to wander around a bit, dear."

"All right. I'll catch up with you later."

Kevin had been fully briefed by his matchmaking wife about Kyra. Now that he'd met the woman, he could see why Patty was so enthusiastic about her.

And he had his instructions.

"Kyra," he said, "there's someone I'd like you to meet. Patty's grandmother."

With his hand in the middle of her back, Kevin guided Kyra to an old woman with a deeply lined face. Her white hair was pulled back and coiled into a bun at the back of her head. Her brown eyes were curious as Kevin and Kyra approached her.

When they reached the older woman, Kevin leaned over and kissed her on the cheek. "Grandmother, I'd like to present Kyra Courtland. She's Jack's new assistant."

Those eyes focused on Kyra with a burning intensity. "How do you do?" There was no handshake. "Is Jack coming?" she asked Kevin.

"He said he was, and you know Jack. He always does what he says."

The old woman nodded. "Yes, he does." She patted the chair beside her. "Sit down, young lady, and keep me company."

Kyra looked toward her aunt and found her in the midst of what appeared to be an interesting conversation with a man about her own age, so she sat next to the woman she knew to be the widow of one of the most powerful Mafia figures in the country.

"How long have you worked with my grandson?"

"Not long."

"Do you enjoy your job?"

"Very much."

The old woman's eyes seemed to examine every inch of Kyra's face. "I saw you with a child when you arrived. Your son?"

"Yes."

"So you're married?" she asked as she looked at Kyra's bare fingers.

"No. Noah is my sister's son. I adopted him when she and her husband died."

Those cool brown eyes suddenly warmed. That was what family was supposed to do. "I can see that you love him very much."

"As though he were my own."

She reached over and covered Kyra's smooth hand with her wrinkled one. "Your nephew will do well with you raising him."

"Thank you."

"Family is the most important thing. People seem to lose sight of that so easily these days."

There was movement near the house. Kyra looked away from Mrs. Allessandro and saw that Jack had arrived with Barbara on his arm. Kevin was making his way toward the couple.

"They make a striking-looking couple," said Kyra.

"Who is that woman?"

"Barbara Wendt."

"Who is she to my grandson?"

"I believe they're seeing each other."

Jack's grandmother sighed.

"What's wrong?"

"My grandson. Sometimes I wonder what he's thinking. Or even *if* he's thinking."

"My mother once told me that men tend to think with parts of their anatomy other than their brains."

The old woman looked at Kyra with twinkling eyes. "My own mother was of the same opinion."

They both studied Jack.

"He doesn't look happy," said Mrs. Allessandro.

Kyra tilted her head slightly as she studied Jack's handsome face almost ten yards away. "I don't know him well enough to tell."

"It isn't his nature to be happy and I know that. He wasn't even that way as a child. But I had hoped things would eventually be different for him. I think if he had a family and settled down, that would help."

"With some men, that only makes them feel more trapped."

"Not my Jack. I think that deep in his soul he longs for that kind of life, whether or not he knows it."

As though sensing their scrutiny, Jack turned his head and looked directly in Kyra's eyes.

Kyra didn't look away but gazed steadily back.

The old woman shifted in her seat as she looked from her grandson to the girl beside her.

This was an interesting turn of events. Maybe Patty was right.

Jack wasn't even aware he was staring at Kyra until Barbara tugged on his arm. "Don't you agree?" she asked.

He turned his head to look at her. "I'm sorry. I didn't hear what you said."

She hugged his arm to her breasts. "Oh, never mind. It isn't important."

He looked back at Kyra and for the first time noticed that she was beside his grandmother. "Come with me, Barbara. There's someone I'd like you to meet."

Arm in arm, they crossed the lawn to where the two women sat.

Kyra started to rise, but Mrs. Allessandro reached out and caught her arm to hold her in place. "You stay right here, dear," she said as her grip relaxed.

Jack and Barbara stopped in front of them. He inclined his head toward Kyra. "I didn't know you were going to be here, Ms. Courtland."

"Ms. Courtland?" interrupted his grandmother. "Goodness, I'm sure there's no need for such formality at a cookout. It should be Kyra and Jack."

Jack smiled with genuine affection at his grandmother as he leaned down to kiss her cheek. "How
are you feeling?"

"Better dear. Thank you." She patted his cheek.

"There's someone I'd like to introduce, Grandmother," Jack said as he moved Barbara forward.

The old woman reluctantly turned her attention to
the redhead on his arm.

"This is Barbara Wendt. Barbara, this is my grandmother, Mrs. Allessandro."

Barbara extended her hand. "I'm so pleased to
meet you."

Mrs. Allessandro dutifully shook Barbara's hand,
but there was no accompanying smile.

At that moment Noah came running toward Kyra
with an older child in hot pursuit. He laughingly flung
himself into Kyra's arms. The older child stopped,
clearly out of breath. "I'm sorry. He got away from
me."

Noah looked up at Jack—way up—and studied his
face with the kind of curiosity only a child can freely
express. "Who's him?"

Noah still didn't have his pronouns quite right.

Jack didn't care. In fact, he smiled as he hunkered
down in front of the child. It was the first smile Kyra
had seen touch his mouth. "Who's *he,* and my name
is Jack. I work with your mother. You must be
Noah."

The little boy nodded. "I'm hungry."

"We can't have that," said Jack. "Let's see if we
can find you something to eat."

Noah moved away from Kyra's arms, and as
though it was the most natural thing in the world, he

wrapped his little hand around one of Jack's fingers, ready to have Jack take him to the food.

Kyra couldn't have been more surprised.

Jack picked up Noah as he rose and lifted him onto his broad shoulders. "Do you like hamburgers?"

"Wots."

"I'm a personal friend of the cook. I bet if we ask him nicely, he'll give us each one." Jack looked at Kyra. "Is that okay with you?"

"Yes, of course."

Noah reached out his hand toward her. "Mama come, too."

"Oh," said Kyra, "I…"

"Yes, do go with them," said Mrs. Allessandro. "Barbara? You sit with me so we can get to know each other a little better."

Barbara looked reluctantly at Jack. She obviously wanted to go with him, but didn't want to be rude to his grandmother.

Manners won out.

As Kyra rose, Barbara took her seat.

"Can we bring either of you back anything?" asked Kyra.

"Not for me, dear," said Mrs. Allessandro. "I'm not hungry just yet."

"Barbara?" asked Kyra.

"No, thank you. I ate before we came."

And so Kyra fell into step with Jack. "You don't have to do this," she said. "I can get Noah food."

He looked into her eyes and…smiled. "I know you can, but he asked me. Right, Noah?"

"Wight."

They arrived at a long table set with everything

from baked beans to potato salad. There were big slices of watermelon and cantaloupe as well as fresh strawberries. It all looked wonderful.

Kevin walked over with a platter of hamburgers and hot dogs. "Here you go. Help yourselves. And don't forget that the games will begin in thirty minutes."

"What games?" asked Kyra.

Patty walked over to her husband and looped her arm through his. "First is the three-legged race. Then pass the orange. And, of course, the egg toss. A badminton game is already going on on the other side of the lawn, and there's volleyball on the beach if you're interested."

"Sounds like fun," said Kyra. "I haven't played any of those games since I was a child."

"Good. Jack can be your partner for the three-legged race. Barbara isn't really dressed for it. And you don't need a partner for passing the orange."

Before she could protest, both Kevin and Patty moved away to talk to another guest.

Still holding Noah, Jack handed the child a plate. "What would you like?"

Noah pointed to a hot dog and Jack fixed one for him. Then Noah pointed at the baked beans and Jack spooned some onto the child's plate. Kyra watched with something between surprise and amusement.

"What?" asked Jack when he noticed her expression.

"I would never have guessed that you would have such a rapport with children."

"Why not?"

"It doesn't fit your outward personality. You're...stern."

"If that's what you think, it would appear that you don't know me very well."

"I don't know you at all."

Jack's eyes met hers for a long moment. There was a warmth in their depths that stirred something in Kyra.

He started to say something, but Noah tugged on his shirt.

Jack looked at her for a moment longer, then set Noah on the ground and turned to fill his own plate.

Kyra did likewise.

Jack inclined his head toward a blanket under a tree. "How about there?"

"Fine."

The three of them made their way to the tree and sat down. Jack stretched his legs out in front of him. Kyra folded her denim-clad legs and Noah just flopped onto the blanket with his little legs circling his plate.

"Perhaps we should go back to your grandmother and Barbara," suggested Kyra as she looked in their direction.

"Oh, no," said Jack. "If I intrude on Grandmother getting to know the woman I'm seeing, I'll never hear the end of it. Better to let their conversation run its natural course."

"So you're close to your grandmother?"

"Very. After my parents died, she raised me until I was sixteen."

"Why just sixteen?"

Jack was silent for a moment. "I finished high school early and was anxious to be out on my own."

Kyra didn't press any further.

"I noticed that you asked your grandmother how she's been feeling. Is she ill?"

"She has a bad heart and it's getting worse. There really isn't anything anyone can do."

"I'm sorry."

"People get old. It happens." The words were casual, but his tone was anything but. He clearly loved his grandmother deeply.

"Bad heart or not, she's still protective of you."

He smiled again. "I know."

"What about your grandfather? Were you close to him as well?"

Jack stretched out on his side and propped himself up on an elbow. "No."

"Why not?"

"Let's just say that we had different philosophies about how life should be lived and business conducted."

"Different in what way?"

"He believed in survival at any cost."

"And you?"

His eyes met hers. "I think there are times when the cost is too high and it's best to fold your tent and go home."

Was he just saying that, or did he really mean it?

Jack looked away from her at the large yard filled with people. Lake Michigan was just a few hundred yards away. It was truly beautiful. And Kyra knew from her files that Jack was the one who had purchased the home and property for his sister.

"Being here almost makes me want to trade in my apartment for a house," Jack said after a moment.

"Almost?"

"My apartment is directly above my office and I don't spend much time there as it is. If I had to get in a car and actually drive home, I'd probably never get there."

"Or you might like it so much you'd look forward to spending more time there."

"Anything is possible."

"But not likely?"

He took a bite of his hamburger as he looked up at her. "I think a house without a family would be a lonely place. More so than an apartment."

"Do you want a family?"

"No."

"Why not?"

"I don't think I'd be very good at being a husband and father, and it's too important to mess up."

"People try and fail all the time. It's a natural part of life. But if a person really wants something and goes after it, more often than not they succeed."

"Your statistics are a little off. More often than not, people fail."

"You wouldn't."

Jack looked at her with a raised brow. "And how do you know that, Ms. Courtland?"

"I can't explain it. There's just something about you that says once you truly fall in love, you'll never veer from that path. And once you have children, you'll be the best father anyone could ask for."

"Thank you for that." He looked into her eyes. "What about you?"

"I'm not missing anything in my life. I have all I need with Noah and my aunt. I love going home at night."

"And that's enough for you?"

"It's what I have."

"So you never wish for more?"

"We talked about this the other night. I try not to."

"What kind of man could tempt you into wishing for more? Or let me guess. The first quality most women say they're looking for is a sense of humor. Is that important to you?"

"I've found that men who make you laugh usually make you cry just as often. I think the main quality I'd look for is maturity, because with that comes trustworthiness, fidelity and a good value system. I want a man I can trust with my heart and with the lives of our children."

"And have you ever found such a man?"

Her eyes moved over his face. "I don't know," she said softly. She realized she was staring at him and abruptly lowered her eyes. "Probably not."

"Probably not? You don't sound very sure of yourself."

"I usually am."

Kyra had no idea how distressed she looked. It caught Jack by surprise. He reached out with his hand and touched her cheek to let her know it was all right.

Kyra's breath caught. She raised her eyes to his.

A frown creased Jack's forehead. Involuntarily he moved his lips closer to hers.

Chapter 8

"Kyra," Jack whispered. "I—"

"Noah!" called the girl who had been watching him earlier.

Kyra jumped.

Jack's hand fell away from her cheek.

The breathless girl dropped to her knees on the blanket next to Noah. "Are you ready for the games?" she asked.

His chin and hands were covered in catsup. "Yeth," he said with a vigorous nod.

Kyra took her napkin and cleaned him up as he squirmed beneath her ministrations. "All done," she said with a smile as she kissed the top of his head.

And then he was off and running to another part of the lawn.

"Finish up," said Jack as he tapped her plate with his index finger. "It's almost time for the race."

"I don't really want to race."

He set his plate aside, took hers from her hands, then rose and pulled her up with him. "Of course you do."

With her hand in his, Jack led Kyra across the lawn to the games area where couples were being tied together with big ribbons. Kevin approached and pushed them closer together. "Come on, Kyra. Put your left leg against Jack's right leg."

She did.

Reluctantly.

Even through their clothing, she felt the electric shock of Jack's touch.

Kevin tied them together at the thigh and again at the ankle. As he straightened, he looked at the two of them. "I'll give you a hint about winning this thing. You need to work as a team. And it helps if you put your arms around each other."

Jack's strong arm went around Kyra's slender waist and held her firmly.

Kyra tried to look game as she put her arm around Jack, but no amount of bravado could disguise her reluctance.

When every pair was tied together, Kevin and Patty lined them up at the starting point. "Ready, set, go!"

Jack and Kyra found their rhythm almost immediately as they took off, their strides perfectly synchronized. They were the first ones across the finish line and instantly lost their balance and fell. Jack caught Kyra in his arms and held her on top of him as they went down, then rolled with her until they stopped, his body half on top of hers. They were both laughing.

But as they looked into each other's eyes, their labored breaths mingling, their racing hearts pressed together, the laughter faded.

Kyra was aware of it all.

Every breath.

Every beat.

She could feel her breasts pressed against his solid chest. Oh, could she feel that, right through to the sensitive core of her body. Her breathing grew more rapid.

Jack made no move to get off of her. Instead, he raised his hand and pushed her hair away from her face. "I think," he said in a deep, soft voice, his eyes on hers, "that our rhythm was very much in sync considering it was our first time," said Jack.

"You mean in the race?"

A corner of his mouth lifted. "What else would I be talking about?"

Kyra's cheeks turned bright pink. "I didn't mean..."

Jack touched his lips with his thumb, silencing her. "In fact, I think we won."

Kyra's heart leaped to her throat. His mouth was so close to hers.

So close.

She could almost feel his lips.

And then Kevin was there, slapping his brother-in-law's back. "Hey, good work, you two!"

Jack looked at her a moment longer, then rolled into a sitting position, bringing Kyra with him. The two of them reached for the ribbon around their thighs at the same moment, their fingers touching.

It was another jolt for Kyra. She jerked her hand back.

Jack took her hand and put it in her lap. As he untied the ribbon, his fingertips lightly brushed against the inside of her thigh.

It wasn't intentional. There wasn't any way to get the ribbon off without touching her.

But that didn't matter.

Kyra closed her eyes as the same feeling of awareness rolled through her body.

Jack noticed, but didn't say anything to her. He handed Kyra the ribbon that had bound their thighs, then undid the one around their ankles and stuffed that one into his own pocket.

After rising, Jack gave Kyra a hand up, letting go as soon as she was on her feet.

Kyra looked anywhere but at him. She was embarrassed by her feelings.

Ashamed.

She had always been in control of herself. Always.

But not with Jack Allessandro.

She had to get away from him to compose herself. At least for a few minutes.

Her reaction was so unprofessional, Kyra couldn't believe it was happening to her.

Emily watched her niece from the sidelines, cheering at first and then growing quiet. There was an expression on Kyra's face she'd never seen before and she found it disturbing.

Kyra tried to distance herself, but Jack wasn't the kind of man who just left a woman standing alone while he wandered away. He put his hand under Kyra's elbow and directed her back toward his grandmother.

Upon their return, Barbara rose so quickly to give

her seat back to Kyra that if Kyra had been in a better frame of mind, it would have been comical.

Mrs. Allessandro's eyes were warmly welcoming, but then she turned them away from Kyra to watch her grandson walk off with Barbara.

"That one," she said under her breath.

"Barbara?"

"And all of the other Barbaras who have come and gone before her. I don't know, Kyra. I've almost given up hope of seeing my grandson happily settled down before I die."

"Stranger things have happened."

"Jack should have children. He's always been good with them," said his grandmother. "It's time for him to have some of his own."

"I'm sure he will someday."

"And you. You should have lots of children."

"I'd like to do something out of the ordinary and get married first."

Mrs. Allessandro laughed. "Yes, we are definitely living in different times than when I was a girl. Are you seeing anyone now?"

"No."

"What a waste of a beautiful young woman!"

Kyra smiled at her. "The next time I'm feeling a little down, I'm going to visit you."

"Any time. And bring Jack."

Just then Kyra made eye contact with her aunt and waved.

"Who is that?" Jack's grandmother asked.

"My aunt. She lives with me and takes care of Noah when I'm at work."

"That's a wonderful arrangement."

"Believe me, I know. I owe her more than I'll ever be able to repay."

Patty ran up to Kyra and abruptly grabbed her hand. "I've been looking all over for you. It's time for pass the orange."

"Oh, Patty, I'd rather stay here and talk to your grandmother, if you don't mind."

"I do," she said as she tugged on Kyra's hand. "Everyone has to play."

Kyra looked at Mrs. Allessandro apologetically. "I'm sorry. Duty beckons."

The old woman nodded and smiled. "You go. I'll be fine here. People watching has long been a hobby of mine."

Patty practically dragged Kyra across the lawn to where two lines of people stood. She pushed Kyra next to Jack.

Jack looked down at Kyra without smiling. "You seem to be a hit with my family. They keep shoving us in each other's path."

"So I gather," she said without enthusiasm. "Sorry about that. It makes things a bit awkward."

"I'm the one who should apologize. They are, after all, mine, not yours."

"I probably shouldn't have come."

"Perhaps not," he said without looking at her, "but I'm glad you did."

"Why?"

A corner of his mouth lifted. "It gave me a chance to meet Noah—and to see a less professional side of you."

As they were talking, the orange slowly made its way toward them. When it finally arrived, Kyra put

her hands behind her back in the traditional fashion
and worked on getting the orange from the man on
her right.

She got it, finally, and turned toward Jack.

Her eyes met his and some of her dread must have
transmitted itself. With more than a little reluctance,
she leaned toward him.

Their eyes held as their faces came closer. Jack's
cheek, lightly shadowed with midday beard, brushed
against hers.

Kyra closed her eyes.

The orange didn't transfer, so they tried again.

Their bodies touched. Kyra's shoulder leaned into
his.

It was a bad angle so she moved directly into him;
her breasts were pressed against his chest.

Her nipples went instantly erect.

She was so aware of the man.

Much to her relief, Jack finally got the orange and
turned to Barbara. Restlessly Kyra stood and waited
for the game to be over with.

When it finally was and their line was the winner,
Kyra politely congratulated the others, including Jack
and Barbara. Just as she had at the office, Barbara
ignored her, turning her head away as Kyra approached.

But Jack smiled at her. "Nice work."

"Thanks."

"Are you sticking around for a while?"

"No. It's been a lovely but long day. I think I
should get Noah and go home. Goodbye."

Kyra turned and walked away to look for her aunt,
but she could feel Jack's eyes on her. She should

probably have hung around and talked to some of the other guests like a good investigator, but she just didn't have the heart for it today.

When she finally spotted Emily, Kyra could see that her aunt was having a lovely time talking to a group of women as they ate, so she left her alone.

Her aunt didn't get out nearly enough, and if they were going to be in Chicago for a few months, she wanted her to have some friends.

Resignedly Kyra wandered around, talking to some of the other guests.

And then she spotted Burton Banacomp. He was walking from group to group, shaking hands. When Patty saw him, she let out a little squeal and ran to hug him. Kevin slapped him on the shoulder. He was clearly beloved by the Allessandro family.

Kyra watched him work the crowd. The man was a born politician. And, in some cases, the people gathered were his constituents. He looked older than his years—older than Jack, she noticed. And he seemed a bit shorter.

Kyra didn't know whether to walk up to him and introduce herself or hang back. She finally decided on anonymity and went to talk to Jack's grandmother again.

The older woman smiled brightly and held out her hands as soon as she saw Kyra. "Hello again, dear. How were the games?"

"Fun. I haven't done anything like that in years."

She nodded. "Patty likes to keep people young. Oh, and look who's here! Burton!"

The congressman walked up to them and took Mrs. Allessandro's hands in his and kissed her on either cheek. "Hello," he said warmly. "You're looking beautiful as always. How have you been?"

"Fine, fine," she answered impatiently. "And how are you?"

"Busy."

"You and Jack. Both of you need a wife and a vacation."

The congressman looked at Kyra with a smile. "She's been trying to marry me off since I was ten." He took Kyra's hand and held it in his. "And you are?"

"Kyra Courtland."

Mrs. Allessandro retrieved his hand from Kyra's. "She's taken."

"I'm sorry to hear that," he said politely. "By anyone I know?"

"Jack."

Kyra's cheeks flushed. "Mrs. Allessandro, please."

"All right," she conceded. "I think she's perfect for him. My grandson appears to have other ideas."

Burton winked at Kyra. "Don't be embarrassed. We're all used to it."

"Yes, but I work for the man," explained Kyra.

"Ah," he said. "I can see how that would make it even worse." A slight frown creased his forehead. "You work for him?"

"As his assistant."

"What happened to Eleanor?"

"She had a better job offer."

"I'm sorry to hear that. I've always enjoyed working with her."

"Are you and Jack in business together?" asked Kyra.

GET A FREE TEDDY BEAR...

You'll love this plush, cuddly Teddy Bear, an adorable accessory for your dressing table, bookcase or desk. Measuring 5 ½" tall, he's soft and brown and has a bright red ribbon around his neck – he's completely captivating! And he's yours *absolutely free*, when you accept this no-risk offer!

▼ CLAIM YOUR FREE BOOKS AND FREE GIFT! RETURN THIS CARD TODAY! ▼

AND TWO FREE BOOKS!

Here's a chance to get **two free Silhouette Intimate Moments® novels** from the Silhouette Reader Service™ **absolutely free!**

There's no catch. You're under no obligation to buy anything. We charge nothing – ZERO – for your first shipment. And you don't have to make any minimum number of purchases – not even one!

Find out for yourself why thousands of readers enjoy receiving books by mail from the Silhouette Reader Service. They like the **convenience of home delivery**...they like getting the best new novels months before they're available in bookstores...and they love our **discount prices!**

Try us and see! Return this card promptly. We'll send your free books and a free Teddy Bear, under the terms explained on the back. We hope you'll want to remain with the reader service – but the choice is always yours!

(U-SIL-IM- 04/98)   **245 SDL CF4T**

NAME

ADDRESS   APT.

CITY   STATE   ZIP

Offer not valid to current Silhouette Intimate Moments® subscribers. All orders subject to approval.

©1993 HARLEQUIN ENTERPRISES LIMITED   **Printed in U.S.A.**

NO OBLIGATION TO BUY!

THE SILHOUETTE READER SERVICE™: HERE'S HOW IT WORKS

Accepting free books places you under no obligation to buy anything. You may keep the books and gift and return the shipping statement marked "cancel", If you do not cancel, about a month later we will send you 6 additional novels, and bill you just $3.57 each, plus 25¢ delivery per book and applicable sales tax, if any.* That's the complete price — and compared to cover prices of $4.25 each — quite a bargain indeed! You may cancel at any time, but if you choose to continue, every month we'll send you 6 more books, which you may either purchase at the discount price...or return to us and cancel your subscription.

*Terms and prices subject to change without notice. Sales tax applicable in N.Y.

"Oh, no." He waved his hand dismissively. "Nothing like that. It's just that Jack and I are old friends. Eleanor had been his assistant for as long as I can remember." He scanned the crowd. "Where is Jack, anyway?"

"If you're going to bother him about business," scolded Mrs. Allessandro, "you can just leave the party this minute."

"Nothing like that," he said as he kissed her cheek again. "Just want to say hi. Excuse me, ladies."

Kyra looked at her watch. She really should be going.

'Don't tell me you're leaving," said the older woman.

Kyra smiled at her and clasped her hand. "It was wonderful meeting you, but I need to gather up my family and head home."

"I hope to see you again, dear."

Though they had just met, Kyra liked the older woman so much. "I'll make a point of it, Jack or no Jack," said Kyra.

"Make sure it's soon. I'm not getting any younger."

With a last squeeze of her frail hand, Kyra walked away. She found her aunt still caught up in an apparently interesting conversation. Then she found Noah playing happily with a group of other young children and being carefully watched by older ones. She wanted to get away. She needed to get away. But something about this family wouldn't let her. She resigned herself to staying for at least another hour.

She walked across the great expanse of green lawn to a sea wall that separated the lawn from the beach and the lake. Perching on top of it, her long legs dangling over the side, she began watching a heated volleyball game on the beach. Jack had joined in. Burton Banacomp, his trousers and shirt sleeves rolled up, was on the opposing side.

But Kyra was more interested in Jack. As she watched, he stripped his shirt off and tossed it on the sand.

Unlike the night in his office, this time Kyra just let herself look as long as she wanted.

He was gorgeous, tanned and muscled and unself-conscious about his body.

And he was athletic. When he jumped for the ball, every muscle in his body strained, and he was a sight to behold.

What must it feel like to be made love to by a man like that?

Not just because of his body, but because of the way he was. So aloof from most people.

What would it be like to get that close to Jack Allessandro? To have him respond to your touch and watch you respond to his?

She closed her eyes for a moment and then opened them again. The ball had rolled away from the players and come to rest near her foot.

Jack ran toward her. As he picked the ball up, he playfully flicked some sand at her.

Kyra smiled at him. She couldn't help herself.

Then Burton called his name.

Jack looked at her for a moment longer, then turned away.

Patty came up behind Kyra and sat on the wall beside her. "Good game?"

"Your brother's team seems to be winning."

"Jack's team always wins. He wouldn't have it any other way."

"So I gather." She turned to the other woman. "Why are you and your husband so bent on throwing us together today?"

Patty looked chagrined. "Is it that obvious?"

"To both Jack and me."

"Oh boy. I'm going to be hearing from Jack about that later, I'm sure."

"I'd count on it if I were you. Which doesn't answer my question. Why are you doing it?"

"I like you," Patty said simply.

"But he already has a girlfriend."

"And I don't like her."

Kyra couldn't help but smile. "It doesn't matter. He does."

The volleyball game ended at that moment and a bunch of sweaty, shirtless men scrambled up the lake bank and over the wall.

Jack, his torso covered in perspiration, his shirt in his hand, stopped in front of his sister. "You and I are going to have a talk when this party is over."

"Jack, I—"

"And Kevin, too. And you might as well apologize to Kyra now and save yourself a phone call." With that, he walked away. The congressman was right beside him.

Patty looked at Kyra and grimaced. "Uh-oh. I guess it's too late to run away from home." Then she shrugged. "Oh, well. He's been mad at me before and I'm sure he will be again. Do you have any brothers or sisters?"

"I had a sister."

"Oh, I knew that. I'm sorry. This just isn't my day. I should have stayed at the hospital."

"That's all right. I don't mind remembering. You're a lot like her."

"Is that good or bad?"

"Very good. I think that's why I'm so comfortable with you."

Patty smiled at Kyra and then spontaneously threw her arms around her. "The heck with Jack. We'll just bypass him and have our own relationship."

Kyra hugged her back, but she was filled with guilt. She liked Patty a lot. In fact, Patty was exactly the kind of person who would have made a wonderful friend. And here Kyra was, lying to her, befriending her under false pretenses while at the same time trying to send her beloved brother to prison.

This job was getting harder and harder. Kyra just wasn't cut out for it any longer. Her heart wasn't in it. She should have never taken this assignment in the first place.

"Well," said Kyra as she looked at her watch. "I should be going now, and this time I mean it. It's getting late and Noah didn't have his nap. He must be really pooped by now." And she knew she'd learned as much about Burton Banacomp as she was going to. At least for now.

"How about this? I'll round up Noah while you get your aunt."

"Thanks, Patty."

Kyra found Emily still contentedly talking to the same group of women. It looked as though a definite bond had been forged, and as Emily said her goodbyes, it sounded as though she had a date for bridge in her future.

"Hello," said Jack quietly as he came up beside her.

Noah was in his arms, his head on Jack's broad shoulder, sound asleep.

"How did this happen?" she asked softly.

"He just climbed onto my lap and fell asleep."

Kyra rested her hand on Noah's back. "He looks so tiny when you hold him."

"That's because he is tiny."

She smiled. "I appreciate your taking care of him, but I've got to take him home now."

"I'll carry him to your car."

"Thank you. You go with my aunt and I'll say our thank-yous and goodbyes."

As Emily and Jack headed for the front yard, she spotted Patty and Kevin and headed toward them.

"I see you found Noah first," said Patty.

"Apparently he found your brother and decided to take a nap without my help." She hugged Patty again and shook Kevin's hand. "Thanks for inviting all of us. We had a wonderful time."

Kevin unexpectedly leaned forward and kissed her cheek. "Now that you know where we live, don't be a stranger. You're welcome here anytime."

"Absolutely," said Patty.

"Thank you. I'll take you up on that. Good night, you two." As she turned away, she looked toward Jack's grandmother's chair. It was empty. She must have gone home. Once again, Kyra's guilt was strong and real.

She wasn't like a smart missile. She couldn't just

hone in on the bad guy. Her investigation was going to leave a lot of collateral damage this time.

She walked quickly around the house to the front. Jack had just finished fastening a still-sleeping Noah into his car seat. As her aunt climbed into the front seat, Kyra stood beside Jack and looked at Noah. "Thank you," she said softly.

"I like your son. He's a good little boy."

Kyra nodded.

Jack opened the driver's door for Kyra and helped her inside. "Drive carefully."

"I will."

"I'll have a driver pick you up on Monday morning around seven to take you to the airport."

"I'll be ready."

"See you then." He looked past her to Aunt Emily. "It was nice meeting you." Then he closed the door and stood in the street as he watched the Jeep drive away.

Jack didn't want to go back to the party but he had to get Barbara and take her home.

Barbara.

Jack sighed.

And then he was going to have a talk with his sister and her husband. This matchmaking nonsense was never going to happen again.

Chapter 9

Kyra rocked slowly in the chair beside the crib as she watched Noah sleep.

"Your ride to the airport is here," whispered her aunt from the doorway.

Kyra sighed. "I hate to leave him."

Her aunt came farther into the room and rested her hand on Kyra's shoulder. "He'll be fine. And you'll only be away for a few days."

"I just miss him so much when I'm gone."

"I know."

Kyra rose from the chair and bent over the crib. For a long moment, she rested her cheek on his, then kissed him lightly. "Goodbye, sweetheart."

Emily followed her niece into the living room and watched as she shouldered her oversize purse.

Through the opened front door, they could see the limousine sitting in the driveway and the uniformed driver lifting Kyra's suitcase into the trunk.

Kyra turned to her aunt and hugged her. "I'll call you."

"Okay, dear. Have a good trip. And don't worry about anything here."

Kyra smiled at her and walked out to the car. The driver inclined his head as he opened the door for her. She climbed inside the spacious car and settled into the back seat. Moments later, the driver smoothly backed out of her driveway and headed for the airport.

The driver wasn't talkative, and Kyra wasn't in the mood for conversation so it was a silent ride.

She had to admit that she was nervous about this trip, nervous about spending so much time with Jack Allessandro.

Before she knew it, the limousine rolled to a stop on the tarmac next to a jet. The driver opened Kyra's door and she slid out.

"I'll stow your luggage, Ms. Courtland."

"Thank you."

She looked at the jet for a few moments, then climbed up the stairs and boarded.

It was nothing if not spacious. There was a table with a large platter of fresh fruit on it. Four comfortable chairs surrounded it. There was also a long couch, perfect for stretching out on, and some other seats that looked like recliners, but with tables so one could work. A VCR and television were built into a wall and there were telephones everywhere.

Kyra moved farther into the jet and found a small but well-stocked kitchen that included a stove, microwave and refrigerator. There was even a shower in the bathroom.

The Department of Justice didn't have anything

like this. At least nothing that they let their operatives fly in.

Suddenly a pilot in uniform came out of the cockpit and smiled at her. "You must be Ms. Courtland."

"Yes."

He walked toward her with his hand extended. "Bill Janson, one of the pilots. We should be taking off in the next fifteen minutes."

"Who else is coming?" she asked.

"Jack, of course, and Barry Chesler."

She looked around the cabin. "Should I sit anywhere in particular?"

"Take your pick."

Kyra decided on one of the side-by-side recliners. As she peered out the window, she saw Jack arriving in one car and Barry in another.

It was Jack she watched as he stood on the tarmac talking to Barry. He was dressed in an immaculate dark suit with a crisp white shirt.

Barry made a sharp gesture with his hand and Kyra suddenly realized that they weren't talking: they were arguing.

Then Jack said something, biting out the words, and Barry, with a shake of his head, walked away from him and boarded the jet.

Barry was still angry, but forced a smile when he saw Kyra. "Hi," he said as he sank into the seat beside her. "Jack didn't tell me you were coming."

"Should he have?"

"Not if he wanted to keep you to himself."

Kyra gave him a long look.

Barry raised his hand in surrender. "Sorry. I was

just trying to make conversation. You're not going to slap me with a lawsuit for flirting, are you?''

"I might if I thought you were serious. But after watching you with other women, it occurs to me that flirting is the only way you know to communicate with the opposite sex.''

"Is there another way?''

"Most women prefer men who speak plainly, without innuendo.''

"Not the women I know.''

"What about your wife?''

"I'm the same man she married five years ago, flirtatious innuendo and all, so she must prefer men who don't speak too plainly. You would appear to be the exception to the rule. So how do I go about talking with you, Kyra Courtland?''

"Try a neutral topic.''

He smiled. "Suddenly I can't think of a thing to say.''

"Then perhaps silence is best,'' she said with a return smile.

"Just a minute,'' said Barry as he looked out the window. "Something is coming to me.'' He seemed to collect his thoughts. "I've got it. Nice weather we've been having lately, don't you think?''

Kyra laughed out loud. "Very nice, indeed.''

"I hope it lasts, but personally I think we're in for more rain before the week is out.''

"I like rain.''

Barry nodded. "Of course you do. Everyone else likes sunshine, so you must like rain.'' He sighed.

"What's wrong?''

"You have to admit that while the weather is an innocuous enough topic, it's boring as hell."

"Incredibly," she agreed.

"So where does that leave us?"

"Without any conversation at all, I'm afraid."

"Maybe. Maybe not. If I asked you how you like your job, what would you say?"

"That I like it very much."

"Why? In essence, you're just a glorified secretary."

"What's wrong with that? It's interesting. So are the people."

"What about the great Jack?"

"What about him?"

"Do the two of you get along all right? He's not exactly overflowing with warmth and good humor."

Kyra turned toward Barry. "You sound as though you don't like him very much."

"He's a great guy. We just have different takes on how business should be done."

"I think I have a general idea of his take," said Kyra. "What's yours?"

"That you get more flies with honey. Jack can be an SOB to work with—not just with his employees, but with customers."

"I wouldn't say that."

"Because you're too diplomatic."

"No. Because I don't think it's true. He might not have your charm, but people always know where they stand with him and I think they appreciate it."

"I'm sure some people do. But the bigger picture is that he chases away a lot of business."

"Give me an example."

"Don't put me on the spot like that."

"You made the statement. I'm just asking you to back it up."

Before Barry could answer, Jack boarded the jet. He nodded in their general direction as he set down his briefcase, then took off his jacket and hung it behind one of the chairs at the table.

Kyra's eyes followed his fingers as he loosened his tie and undid the top button of his shirt.

Barry left the chair and walked over to Jack. "Are you going to work on the numbers?"

"I should have something finished by the time we land."

"You're going to have to be reasonable. If you're not, you'll lose the business."

Jack looked straight at Barry. "I'm always reasonable. But not so much that I'll be made a fool of. Bringing tankers full of oil and scrap to Spain is one thing. Sending them back to the Middle East empty is foolish and wasteful, and that's what we've had to do for the past year. If we can't find someone who wants to ship something on the return voyage, then I say we should let the business go completely."

"And do what? Let the tankers sit at the docks empty?"

"If need be."

Barry shook his head. "I don't know why you're being so stubborn about this. Things have been fine for a year, and then all of a sudden you want to make changes."

Jack leaned back in his seat. "And I don't know why you're so interested in the business end of things. That's my job."

Once they were airborne, Kyra

"If this is an example of the decisions you've been making, then maybe it's time I get involved."

Jack was completely unruffled. "Barry, if you don't want to be a part of this company anymore, I'll buy you out."

"You couldn't afford my price."

"Try me."

Barry shook his head. "Sometimes there's no dealing with you, Jack. You think you have all the answers."

Kyra decided it was time to break the tension between the men. "Excuse me. Is there anything you want me to do while we're en route to Spain?"

Jack stared at Barry for a moment, then looked at Kyra. "Just relax for now. Read a book. We have a dinner tonight after we land, so you're going to have a long day."

"I'm used to it."

Barry was still angry. It showed in his body language as he walked to a closet, got a pillow and blanket, then settled into the recliner next to Kyra. "I had a late night," he said by way of explanation. "As a matter of fact, I haven't been home yet, so excuse me while I catch a few z's."

And just like that, before the plane had left the ground, he was sound asleep.

Kyra watched Jack as the plane taxied down the runway. He was sitting at the table, his sleeves rolled halfway up his strong forearms. His briefcase was open, a computer not yet turned on in front of him. He was writing something on a notepad.

He didn't even look up as the jet took off.

Once they were airborne, Kyra left her chair and

took a seat across from him. "Are you sure I can't help?"

Jack raised his head. "If you really want to work, there's always a lot to do."

"That's why I'm here."

He turned his computer toward her. "We're at a high enough altitude to turn it on."

She pressed the power button. "Now what?"

He gave her a series of instructions that connected her with the company computer—including his password.

She could hardly believe it.

He had her moving in and out of files, changing things here, corresponding there, E-mailing employees, writing letters. They worked steadily for several hours.

Finally Jack leaned back in his seat and stretched his arms over his head. "Let's take a break," he said as he rose and headed for the kitchen. "Can I get you something to drink?"

"Diet soda."

"Not a coffee drinker, are you?"

"Can't stand it. How did you know?"

"I've never seen a cup on your desk." He disappeared for a minute, then returned with two sodas and one glass with ice. "Barbara lives on coffee."

Kyra popped open her can and she poured its contents into her glass. "How did she like the bracelet?"

Jack took a long drink out of the can as he looked out the window. "Considering it was a goodbye gift, I think she liked it well enough."

"Oh," said Kyra in surprise. "I wasn't aware of that when you asked me to buy it."

"Neither was I. That's just the way it worked out."

"I'm sorry."

"Don't be. I'm not."

He set down the can and leaned forward. "Let's get back to work."

And they did, all the way to Barcelona.

At the airport, the three of them deplaned then immediately climbed onto a helicopter and flew to Costa Azul, where they landed on the roof of an absolutely beautiful hotel on the Mediterranean.

"Why aren't we staying in Barcelona?" asked Kyra as Jack helped her from the helicopter. "That's where your freighters are."

"Because this is nicer. Cleaner. I'll visit the shipyards tomorrow."

"Am I going on that trip?"

"It's not necessary, but you can, if you like."

"I would like to. Thank you."

They didn't even have to check in. They simply took a private elevator to the ground floor. It opened into a private bungalow.

"I keep a place here permanently," Jack said by way of explanation as they walked from the large foyer into the main living area where there was an open bar and kitchen. It was light and airy, full of sunshine.

Barry crossed the room and walked ahead of them through a pair of double doors that led to a bedroom. "That's where Barry sleeps," said Jack. "I'm over there." He pointed at another set of double doors. "And Ms. Hanover slept there," he said as he pointed at yet another set of doors. "I assume you'll have no problem with staying here."

"Of course not."

"Good. I also have an office here, but I rarely use it." He looked at his watch. "We have exactly one hour before we leave for dinner. Meet me back here in fifty-five minutes."

Kyra looked at her watch. "All right. Formal or informal."

"Something like what you were wearing the other night will be fine."

"How about something exactly like what I was wearing? Some of us don't have your budget."

A corner of Jack's mouth lifted. "You can wear it however often you like, Kyra."

She liked the way her name sounded when he said it. "I'll see you shortly," she said.

Kyra went to the bedroom Jack had pointed toward. Stopping in the doorway, she looked around in appreciation. It was done in different creamy hues and natural woods with almost no contrasting colors. The result was a beautiful blend that made the room seem larger and brighter than it was. French doors led to the terrace, as they did in the living room.

"Excuse me, ma'am," said a man's voice in Spanish.

Kyra turned to find a uniformed bellhop standing in the open doorway with her suitcase.

"Where would you like me to put this?"

"On the bed, please."

He hoisted it up and turned to leave.

"Here," said Kyra, digging into her purse for some money.

"No," he said with a bow. "Please. It has all been taken care of."

She put her money back. Jack. He took care of everything.

Kyra took a quick shower. Then, wrapped in a towel, she opened her French doors and let the breeze from the sea lift the filmy drapes and send them billowing into the room.

She could learn to live like this.

Humming softly to herself, she opened her suitcase and unpacked, hanging her skirt suits neatly in the closet and her three dinner dresses, still in their cleaning bags, next to them.

Jeans, a sweater, pajamas and underwear went into her drawer.

Then she unpacked her toiletries.

Kyra reapplied what little makeup she usually wore, then pulled her silky hair away from her face and into its usual neat twist. But tonight she playfully pulled a few strands loose and let them frame her face and curl on the back of her neck.

She decided on the black mandarin dress she'd worn before because she felt like wearing black and it was the only black dress she'd brought. And, just like before, she couldn't get it zipped all the way.

Jack was going to have to help her again.

When she had on her high heels, Kyra looked herself over in the full-length mirror. Elegantly businesslike. Exactly what she wanted.

Leaving her purse behind, she opened her door and walked into the main living area. At first she thought that Jack wasn't there, but then she saw him through the open French doors, leaning on the railing of the terrace, looking out at the sea.

Kyra came up behind him. "Nice view."

Jack nodded without looking at her.

"Why don't you live here all the time?"

"My family is in Chicago."

She understood perfectly.

Jack turned his head and smiled when he saw what she had on. "You weren't joking."

"I like this dress," she said defensively.

Straightening away from the railing, he turned her around. With a gentle tug, he zipped up the dress the rest of the way. "How do you usually get out of it?" he asked, amused.

"My aunt helps me."

"Not this time."

"I guess I'll have to depend on the kindness of strangers—or sleep in it, one or the other. Who are we having dinner with tonight?"

"Jose Zamora and his son, Franco."

Kyra involuntarily winced.

"Do you know them?"

"The son more than the father."

"It doesn't sound as though it's a happy acquaintance."

"I offered Franco friendship, and he wanted something more. It took a long time for him to turn his interest in other directions. And even then I had to lie about being involved with someone else."

"If he bothers you tonight, tell me and I'll take care of it."

And Kyra knew he would.

"Shall we go?"

"What about Barry?" she asked as they went inside and headed for the elevator.

"Coming!" said Barry as he closed his doors and fell into step behind them.

They went up one floor to the main lobby and walked straight through to a limousine that was waiting in the drive.

Kyra climbed in first.

Barry sat beside her and Jack across from her.

She gazed out the window as they traveled inland, away from the water, but she was intensely aware of Jack's eyes on her the entire trip.

They stopped about fifteen minutes later at a small but elegant-looking restaurant.

Jack climbed out first and took Kyra's hand to help her.

She looked up at him as she stepped out. "Thank you."

He unsmilingly inclined his dark head.

As soon as they walked inside, the maître'd greeted both Jack and Barry by name and offered Kyra a polite nod. "Your guests have already arrived," he said as he showed them into the dining room, guiding them around the heavily occupied dance floor to a rear table that was more quiet and private than the others.

Kyra saw Franco Zamora before he saw her. He was as handsome as she remembered: tall, lean and dark, with eyes that could devour you with their intensity. She was reminded of why she'd been drawn to him in the first place.

And why he'd begun to frighten her later on.

When they noticed the arrival of their hosts, he and his equally handsome father both rose at the same time.

Franco greeted the men first, then his eyes fell on
Kyra. His friendly smile faded and then grew into a
delighted grin. "Kyra?" he asked as he looked more
closely at her.

"Hello, Franco," she said politely.

"It *is* you!" He walked around the table to take
both of her hands in his. "I can hardly believe it.
What's it been now—four years? Five?"

"Five, I think."

"You remember Kyra Courtland, don't you, Father?"

Jose nodded his large head as he looked at her from
beneath bushy black eyebrows. "Of course. I was
very sorry to hear of the death of your father. He was
a good man."

"Thank you."

"Please," said Jose, "let's all take our seats and
be comfortable."

Franco made sure Kyra was seated just to his right,
but Jack stayed with her, making sure he was seated
on her other side. Barry sat between Jose and Jack.

"What will you have to drink?" asked Jose Zamora, as though he were the host. "Kyra?"

"Dry sherry."

Franco smiled. "I remember your liking that. It's
what you always had at your father's parties." He
touched her hand. "Tell me about yourself, Kyra.
When I tried finding you after that last time we spoke,
it was as though you'd fallen from the face of the
earth. How did you manage to disappear so completely?"

She politely pulled her hand away and placed it in
her lap. "You must have looked in the wrong places.

It's nearly impossible for anyone to disappear these days.''

"I heard that you went to work for the government after your father's death.''

Kyra looked at him in what she hoped appeared to be mild surprise. "I can't imagine who would have told you that.''

"Claire Adams.''

She had been Kyra's best friend all those years ago.

"I'm sure that's what she said.'' He looked skyward as though trying to recall exactly what he'd heard. "The State Department—or perhaps it was the Justice Department. I don't remember precisely.''

"Claire was mistaken.''

"She seemed quite certain.''

"It was a long time ago, Franco. I imagine things have grown fuzzy over the years.''

"Actually, I had investigators checking all over Washington for you.''

Kyra's identity had been obscured by the Justice Department since the day she'd signed on as an investigator, so she could make the next remark with complete confidence. "And they didn't find me, did they?''

"No. And when they checked the rest of the country, they didn't find you there, either.''

He had her there. All of her legal documents, including taxes, were changed to her mother's maiden name. "I was in Virginia, working at a private corporation.''

"What corporation would that be?''

"Hennessey, Inc. It's a fairly small company.''

Franco nodded his head. "Well, the next time I see

Claire, I'll have to tell her I found you. Or, rather, you found me." He looked at Jack. "So now you're working for this fellow."

"That's right."

"So what exactly do you do for Jack?"

"I'm his assistant."

Franco continued to stare at Jack, who appeared to be paying attention to what Jose Zamora was saying to him rather than the conversation between the two of them.

"Are you happy where you are?"

"Very."

His gaze shifted to Kyra. "I wouldn't have thought it possible, but you've grown even more beautiful."

"Thank you," she said expressionlessly.

"I was so in love with you."

"I know. I'm sorry I couldn't return your feelings."

"Me, too." He shrugged. "But that was then and this is now. We're both different people."

"Some things haven't changed, Franco."

He didn't seem to be listening. "Why did you lie to me about seeing another man when I wanted to date you?"

Kyra sighed inwardly.

"I asked you a question," he said more firmly.

She turned her head to look at him directly. "Because I told you time and time again that I didn't want to go out with you, but you wouldn't listen. I thought that if I made up a boyfriend, you'd be able to back away from me and save face."

"That's pretty blunt."

"You apparently won't be satisfied with anything less."

"Are you seeing anyone now?"

Before she could answer, Jack put his arm along the back of her chair. As he spoke with the elder Zamora, his fingers absently toyed with a soft curl that had come loose from her twist. It was a nothing gesture, yet carried with it a certain intimacy that Franco saw and Kyra felt. She understood that Jack was quietly helping her.

At its heart, the action was impersonal. But that didn't change the way Kyra's sensitive skin reacted to Jack's touch.

And it silenced Franco.

Kyra tried to focus her thoughts on what was being said among the men. But at the same time she was incredibly aware of Jack's light touch, almost to the exclusion of any other awareness.

Focus. Focus. She repeated it like a mantra.

Then Jack took his hand away and suddenly she could concentrate again.

The conversation had started out as small talk, but quickly turned serious, even before dinner was served.

"What I'm looking for," said Jose, "is a long-term contract with your company to shuttle my scrap and petroleum between the Middle East, China and Barcelona. The one we currently have with you is set to expire in six weeks."

"I know that," said Jack. "And I want to keep your business, but not at a fixed price and not without some kind of return shipment when we go back for the next tankerful."

"I can't do anything about your return shipments,"

said Jose. "That's for you to work out. But just from an oil perspective, look at it this way—if there's a shortage or an embargo, you'll make out like a bandit."

"And if there isn't and my fuel, labor and insurance prices go up—and you know they always do—then I barely break even. I'm in this business to make money, Jose. I can do nothing and break even."

"For the kind of money I'm offering you, isn't it worth the risk to sign a long-term contract?"

Barry turned to Jack and, rather undiplomatically for a business partner, said, "I think it is. Either way, we lose nothing."

Jack was unswayed, though. "I want to continue our relationship, Jose," he said. "And I'm certainly willing to compromise on our current contractual terms, but you're going to have to compromise, as well."

"How much?" asked Jose.

"I want to have my people make their own projections about supply and demand and where the political winds are blowing. And I also want to get the figures on sending back those empty tankers. It costs more than it used to."

"Of course."

"It'll take time."

"I understand."

Franco leaned forward and tapped his forefinger on the table for emphasis. "But not too much time. You're not the only shipping company out there. And I think this thing about sending back empty tankers is a nonissue. I'm sure we can work something out about that."

"Franco!" said Jose in a reprimand so loud it was very nearly a shout.

Franco fell instantly silent.

Jack looked at Franco for a long moment, then addressed himself to Jose. "I'll have the numbers to you in a week, and you can count on them being fair."

"I've done business with you long enough to know that," said Jose with a smile. "But fair or not, they're still negotiable."

"Everything is negotiable," said Barry.

A woman came up behind Barry at that moment and put her hands on his shoulders. "Barry? What a delicious surprise!" she said in a cultured British accent. "I didn't know you were going to be here."

Barry looked over his shoulder with a sudden smile, stood and embraced the woman. "Angela, how are you?"

"Much better now. I was expecting to pass a deadly dull week with my friends, but with you in town, things are definitely looking brighter." She looked around the table. "Aren't you going to introduce me?"

"Of course. I'm sorry." He went around the table with the introductions.

Her eyes rested briefly on Jack—what woman's wouldn't?—then returned to Barry as soon as he'd finished. "Would you care to dance, darling?"

He looked at Jack. "I'd say our business here is pretty much concluded, wouldn't you?"

Jack looked at Jose.

The older man nodded in agreement. "There's nothing more to discuss. The next move is yours."

Barry clapped his hands together. "All right, then.

If you'll excuse me, I'm going to start the fun part of my evening.''

Franco rose and turned to face Kyra. ''Let's dance.''

Before Kyra could decline, Jack took her hand in his and pulled her to her feet. ''I'm afraid she's already promised this one and all that follow to me.''

She smiled gratefully at him as he escorted her onto the parquet floor with the other couples. ''Thank you.''

''I could see you were anxious,'' said Jack as he pulled her into his arms. ''I've got him thinking we're in a relationship without actually saying the words. If you want me to back off on that, I can undo it.''

''No! Please. The man has a stalker mentality. I don't want to have to deal with him again.''

''Fair enough. But I have to tell you,'' he said with a half smile, ''you're not acting like a woman in love. Or even one just having a fling, for that matter.''

As they danced, she was holding her body at what she considered a safe distance from his. ''Do you think he'll notice?'' she asked, concerned.

''He's been watching you like a hawk all evening,'' said Jack. ''Of course he'll notice.''

''Sorry.'' Kyra moved a little closer.

Jack shook his head as he pressed his hand against the middle of her back, bringing her body into direct contact with his.

Her head came up abruptly in surprise.

''Much better,'' he said quietly. ''It would probably be even more effective if you'd stop looking so surprised.''

Kyra quickly changed her expression to a more neutral one.

"Not great, but it will do," Jack said. He bent his head and leaned his forehead against hers.

"What are you doing?"

He kissed the outer corner of her eye. "Behaving the way a lover would when he's dancing with his woman."

"I don't know about this."

He kissed the spot where her dimple appeared when she smiled. "Isn't this what lovers do when they dance?"

"I'm not big on public displays of..."

Jack kissed the sensitive spot just in front of her ear.

Her breath came out in a rush. "Affection." Kyra could feel the warmth of his lips; hear the soft sound of his breath.

Jack felt a tremor run through her body. Raising his head slightly, he pulled her closer and moved slowly with the music. "All right. No public displays."

Kyra didn't want to talk. She just wanted to feel every movement of his body against hers.

Her body responded of its own volition to the slightest pressure of his hand on her back.

And his body responded to her.

Kyra raised her head and looked into Jack's eyes. She knew she wasn't alone in what she was feeling. She started to speak.

But Jack gently touched her lips with his fingers. "No," he said softly. "Just dance."

She looked at him a moment longer, then put her cheek on his shoulder until the music died away.

Chapter 10

Barry maneuvered his way through the couples on the dance floor until he got to Jack and Kyra. "I'm going to split for the evening," he said with a look in Angela's direction that left very little to the imagination. "I assume I can leave the Zamoras in your capable hands, partner."

From his tone, Barry seemed to have gotten over his earlier argument with Jack, Kyra noted.

Jack stopped dancing, but his arm was still around Kyra. "Go ahead. Our business is finished."

"And don't expect me back tonight. I'll see you tomorrow, probably late."

With a wink at Kyra, Barry was gone.

"It must be hell being married to him," she said as she watched him walk away.

"Probably."

"Do you think his wife knows what he does?"

"He doesn't exactly hide it."

"Then why does she put up with it?"

"Perhaps because she loves him, despite everything."

"That's not love," she said sadly. "It's something else entirely."

"I take it you wouldn't tolerate that kind of behavior from your husband?"

"I wouldn't have to because I could never love a man like that." Her eyes met his. "If you were married, you'd never sleep with a woman other than your wife." Kyra was absolute in her conviction.

"How do you know that?"

"I just do."

"Even though in the past I've slept with women I haven't loved?"

"It's not the same thing," said Kyra.

Jack smiled slightly as he raised his hand to her face and cupped her cheek. "You're an idealist," he said.

Kyra's smooth, cool hand settled gently over his as she looked into his eyes. "If you knew me better, I'm afraid you'd discover that deep in my heart, I'm quite cynical."

They began swaying in time to the music again.

As Kyra looked over Jack's shoulder, she caught sight of Barry entwined with Angela, kissing deeply, neither of them caring that people were watching.

Jack suddenly swung her around. "Let's say goodnight to the Zamoras and go home."

Taking her hand, Jack led her through the dancers to their table. Jose was sitting alone.

Kyra tried to find Franco in the crowd of diners and dancers, but had no luck.

Jack leaned over Jose as the older man rose. "I want to keep your business. As I said, I'll run the numbers and get back to you."

"Soon."

"Count on it. Can my driver drop you anywhere?"

"I have my own, thank you. I enjoyed dinner, Jack."

"My pleasure."

Jose turned to Kyra and bent low over her hand. "It was a pleasure seeing you again."

"And you," she said politely.

As they turned to walk away, Jack put his arm snugly around her waist, holding her close to his side.

Kyra could feel her body heat rising.

She suddenly stopped walking and looked up at Jack. "I'd like to go to the ladies' room before we leave."

"Of course."

She excused herself and disappeared through the nearby door. As soon as she was in the connected powder room, she sat on a stool in front of a mirror and stared at herself. Her cheeks were bright pink. She pressed her fingertips against her hot skin.

Rising from the stool, she went into the next room and ran some cold water over her hands, then pressed them against her cheeks, repeating the process until she could feel her skin begin to cool.

Taking some tissues in her hands, she patted her cheeks dry and looked in the mirror again. She wasn't as flushed as she had been, but her heart was still racing.

Picking up her purse, she took a deep breath, straightened her posture and walked with a confidence she didn't feel through the door and into the restaurant.

Jack wasn't there.

She looked around and finally spotted him at the bar laughing at something Franco said to him.

She couldn't believe it. They'd practically ignored each other during dinner and now they were at the bar laughing?

Then they put their heads closer together and spoke more seriously. Kyra just watched.

It didn't necessarily mean anything.

She watched a moment longer, then went back into the ladies' room. She did a slow count to a hundred and then exited again.

Jack was there.

As he looked at her, a corner of his mouth lifted. ''Hello.''

Kyra's heart hammered against her breast. A look and a word from the man was all it took.

He put his hand at her waist as they walked out of the restaurant to wait for his car. Once they were outside, Kyra stepped away from him.

''What's wrong?'' Jack asked.

''Nothing. It's just that we don't need to continue the pretense. Franco is nowhere around.''

Jack gazed at her profile. ''I see.''

Where was the car? she wondered impatiently as she crossed her arms under her breasts and shifted her weight from one foot to the other.

When it finally stopped in front of them, Jack

opened the door and gave Kyra a hand into the car, then climbed in himself and sat facing her.

"What do you think of the Zamoras?" he asked.

"I like Jose. I always have."

"And Franco?"

Kyra lifted her shoulders.

"Come on. You have an opinion on everything and everyone."

"All right. He scares me a little. But in a personal way, not business."

"I can understand your being irritated at him, but why does he scare you?"

"There's a meanness in him. A repressed violence."

"And yet you went out with him."

"Once. I was reacting to the handsome package. But it only took one date for me to figure out I didn't like the contents."

"It looks as though he didn't come away from that date with the same negative feelings."

"Apparently not."

She leaned her head against the back of the seat and looked out the car window. It was dark outside. There were no streetlamps to light their way and very little moonlight.

Her hands fidgeted nervously in her lap.

Jack leaned back, too, and stretched out his long legs.

They rode in an uncomfortable silence.

Jack gazed at Kyra's profile in the dim glow of the interior's recessed lights. There was a timeless quality to her beauty. She could have fit into any century and held her own.

He even felt a little sorry for Franco. It was easy to understand how having Kyra could become a man's obsession.

He turned his head away.

Kyra couldn't shake her feeling of unease. She was hypersensitive to everything around her—sounds, scents, voices…even silence. She was filled with a feeling of apprehension that made her want to bolt from the car.

When finally they stopped in front of the hotel, that was very nearly what she did.

Before the driver or Jack could even reach for the door, Kyra had it open and was standing on the pavement under the canopy.

Jack looked at her strangely. "Would you like to have a drink before we turn in?"

"No, thank you." Her edginess was evident in her voice. "I just want to go to sleep."

He handed her a key card to use in the elevator. "Keep that one. I have another."

"All right."

"See you in the morning."

"Good night," she said without looking at him.

As Kyra hurried away, Jack's eyes followed her until she was out of sight.

Kyra repeatedly pressed the elevator button, as though the action would make it come faster. As soon as the doors opened, she climbed on board and inserted her key card, then waited anxiously while it made the trip down one floor.

She went straight to her room and closed the door. Kicking off her shoes, she reached behind her to unzip her dress. She managed to get it part of the way, but couldn't budge those few inches out of her reach.

"Ahh!" she growled in frustration.

Reaching behind with both of her hands, she yanked on the dress and ripped it the rest of the way, then pushed it down over her hips and kicked it away from her.

Her hair. That was next. She couldn't stand having it pulled back for one more minute. Out of the twist it came. She shook it free and let it fall in a wave to her shoulders.

With fingers so impatient they were awkward, she pulled off her stockings and underwear, snatched her usual T-shirt and boxers out of a drawer and put them on.

She still felt confined.

She started to take out her contacts, but changed her mind and left them in.

She paced around her room, and when even that didn't help, she opened her terrace doors and stepped outside, thinking that the vastness of the sand and sea would help release this feeling that filled her to the bursting point. She could see down the terrace past the living area and Barry's room, but Jack's was around the corner, out of sight.

She leaned on the railing and raised her face to the sky.

She had to calm down.

Take deep breaths. Exhale slowly.

Breathe. Exhale.

Jack walked into the dark suite. He glanced toward Kyra's door and paused for a moment before walking into his own room and closing the door.

Without turning on the light, he stripped out of his shirt, tossed it aside, then lay on his bed, his hands behind his head, and stared at the ceiling.

Ever since Kyra had come into his life, she was all he could think about.

Her face was the only one he could see.

He wanted to talk to her.

Look at her.

Touch her.

Be with her.

Jack sat up and dragged his fingers through his hair. There was no way he was going to be able to sleep tonight.

With only his trousers on, Jack went outside to the terrace and stared at the sea.

It wasn't working. Nothing Kyra did calmed her.

And she wasn't about to go back into her room. She would go crazy.

Running. That was the answer. She would go for a long, hard run on the beach.

In her bare feet, she took off down the terrace and rounded the corner. She didn't see Jack standing there, but he'd heard her coming and caught her in his arms just as she would have crashed headlong into him.

They just looked at each other.

Without a word from either of them, their lips met in a crushing kiss. Kyra's arms went around his neck, literally hanging on to Jack as he lifted her off her feet. She wrapped her legs around his waist as he carried her inside his room and pressed her back against a wall.

They were beyond rational thought.

All Kyra knew was what she felt, and what she felt was Jack's throbbing desire pressed against her and her own white-hot need to have him inside her.

Her boxers hit the floor. And suddenly he was.

Kyra gasped as Jack entered her, but it was a gasp of sheer pleasure. She wrapped her legs even more tightly around him, pulling him closer with each thrust.

Jack couldn't hold back, but it didn't matter. They climaxed together in an explosion of passion unlike anything they'd ever known.

Kyra buried her face in his neck to muffle her scream.

Jack continued to move inside of her even after they had peaked. Their bodies were wracked with aftershocks.

His breathing ragged, Jack carried Kyra to the bed and they both collapsed on top of it, still in each other's arms.

They just lay there silently, unable to speak.

Then Jack raised himself over Kyra and looked into her eyes. She was, to him, the most beautiful woman he'd ever seen. He kissed the corner of her mouth, then gently captured her lips with his, kissing her with a lingering tenderness.

Kyra kissed him back with softly responsive lips. The nervous energy that had plagued her throughout the evening was gone, replaced with an almost dead calm.

Jack lifted the T-shirt she still had on and pulled it

over her head, tossing it aside. Lowering his mouth to her shoulder, he caressed her skin with his lips, moving them over every inch of her, teasing her body to life again with his tongue.

He brought her to the brink again and again, then finally entered her and began moving with a rhythmic slowness.

Kyra wrapped her legs around him, holding him inside her.

Jack raised himself up on his forearms so he could look at her flushed face as he thrusted slowly. He watched as this usually controlled woman lost control again. His thrusts grew harder and deeper until once again they both climaxed.

He rolled onto his back, taking Kyra with him. Her cheek rested on his shoulder, her hand on his rock-hard stomach.

"Jack," she whispered.

"Shh," he said as he kissed her hair and stroked the soft skin of her arm. "Let's not talk. There'll be time for that tomorrow. Let's just enjoy the moment."

Kyra stared into the darkness.

Oh my God. What had she done?

The sun hadn't yet risen when Kyra awoke, still in Jack's arms.

Carefully, so as not to disturb Jack, she raised herself on her elbow and gazed at the sleeping man. Dark beard shadowed his cheeks, covering the grooves that formed when he smiled.

His mouth. What could she say? It was a mouth women would be drawn to—sculpted, full...yet not too full. Just looking at it sent a shiver of desire through Kyra because she now knew just what that mouth could do to a woman's body.

Her body.

His lashes were dark and surprisingly long, and they formed a half-moon over his closed eyes.

He looked utterly at peace.

But Kyra knew that all she had to do to arouse Jack was to touch him, kiss him. It would be last night all over again.

She closed her eyes and let the warmth of the night before fill her once again. She reached out her hand, almost but not quite touching him.

And then she opened her eyes.

Slowly…reluctantly…regretfully, she withdrew it.

She had no right. This man had no idea who she was. If he had, he never would have made love to her.

What if he were innocent? And she believed more and more that he was. What was he going to think when he found out that she was an impostor? That she was willing to lie to the extent that she allowed last night to happen? Would he ever believe that her feelings had been real? That she hadn't used sex to get closer to him just to get information?

No matter what she had felt, no matter how sincere her feelings and desire for him had been, to Jack it would be the biggest betrayal of all when he found out she was investigating him.

And however this case turned out, Jack was going to learn who she really was.

And if he was innocent, she had utterly deceived him.

She felt ill.

Kyra climbed out of bed with as little movement as possible, pulled her oversize T-shirt on and padded across the suite to her own room. After she was showered and dressed, she went in search of a public phone. There were times when she simply didn't risk using a cellular.

She found one in the lobby of the hotel and promptly made a collect call to Riley's home.

Half a world away, Riley looked blearily at the numbers on his digital clock even as he lifted the receiver. "Whoever this is, do you have any idea what time it is?"

"It's me, Riley," said Kyra.

He sat up straight. "Kyra? Where are you calling from?"

"A pay phone in Costa Azul."

"What's going on? You sound odd."

Kyra paused as she took a deep breath. "You have to take me off this case, Riley."

"Whoa, there. Wait up. We've talked about this already. I can't take you off."

"You have to. I've made too big a mess of things."

"What are you talking about?"

A hot tear rolled down Kyra's cheek. "I'm too close to things."

Riley was puzzled for a moment, but then the cloud cleared. "Oh, Kyra, tell me you didn't sleep with him."

Kyra said nothing.

"Ohh," groaned Riley. "Kyra, you of all people. You've never done anything like this before. What were you thinking? What kind of credibility are you going to have as a witness against Allessandro when his attorney throws this little nugget into the mix?"

Tears stung the backs of Kyra's eyes. "You're right. You're absolutely right. That's why you have to take me off this case right now."

Riley took the phone away from his ear for a moment while he thought.

"Riley?"

He raised the phone. "No."

"You aren't listening to me, Riley. For heaven's sake, I slept with the man!"

"I know, I know. But we might be able to use this to our advantage."

"What?" She was genuinely shocked.

"You've certainly gotten his attention and probably his trust."

"Oh, no. Don't even go there, Riley."

"Wait a minute. Hear me out. You might have tainted yourself as a witness, but the facts you dig up will speak for themselves. We can hang this guy out to dry."

"What if he's not doing anything wrong?"

"He is. I can smell it."

"I've watched him deal with people, Riley. I don't think he's the kind of man who would smuggle technology or arms to make a few extra bucks."

"You don't *think?* We should drop the entire investigation because you don't *think* he'd do it? We're not talking about a few dollars, kid. We're talking about millions. And he's an Allessandro. Good God, woman, where's your objectivity?"

That got her hackles up. "Oh, and *you* are being objective? You want to pin this on him whether he's guilty or not, just because he's an Allessandro. You were never able to nail his grandfather, so you're go-ing after Jack.''

Riley was startled into silence. Kyra had never spo-ken to him with such anger. ''You've certainly grown defensive about him,'' he said more quietly.

''I'm not defensive. I've just gotten to know him better.''

''That's an understatement,'' Riley said under his breath.

Kyra inhaled deeply and slowly exhaled. ''Riley, I'm telling you that we're looking at the wrong per-son. Jack is an honorable man. He would never, ever, do anything to put his country in jeopardy.''

Riley was silent.

''You've always trusted my instincts before. Why is this time different?''

''Because you're too close to Allessandro to see him for what he is.''

''I can't change that now. What do you want me to do? Pack it in and come home?''

Kyra was completely unaware that Jack had en-tered the lobby and was standing at the far end, watching her.

''Hell, no. There isn't another person I can get as close to Allessandro as you are anytime soon. More lives—possibly those of American soldiers—will be lost if we don't put an end to this. And I don't even want to think about our national security. If—and you'll notice that I said 'if'—Allessandro is guilty, I want him stopped and nailed. All the information we have at DOJ so far points right at him. That's not me talking, Kyra. Those are the facts. If that information is wrong or if there's new information pointing somewhere else, I need to know that and I need to know it yesterday. Your personal feelings about the man aren't relevant. You need to set them aside and get on with your job. Do you read me, Kyra?''

Kyra sighed.

''You messed up. Big time. But it's not irreparable. We can still salvage this operation. And if you're so sure the man is innocent, prove it to me!''

Kyra leaned her forehead against the plastic rim around the phone booth.

''And if he's guilty, he deserves whatever he gets. Are you with me, Kyra?''

''I don't have a choice, do I?''

''No, Kyra, you don't. Not if you want a career at the DOJ. You know how fond I am of you, but even I won't be able to save your job if you mess up this assignment because you got personally involved. I'm sorry.''

''Yeah, so am I. I'll be in touch. Goodbye, Riley.''

As she hung up the phone, hands came down on her shoulders. Kyra nearly jumped out of her skin as she spun around to find Jack standing there.

''Why are you using the pay phone instead of the one in the room?''

Kyra thought fast. ''I was walking through the lobby and decided on the spur of the moment to call home.''

''At this hour?''

''I forgot what time it was in Chicago. My aunt reminded me.''

Jack looked at her more closely. If there was one thing he knew, Kyra hadn't been calling home. He'd watched her for quite a while from across the lobby and had seen anger, frustration, hurt and resignation. There was no way she'd been talking to either Noah or her aunt. She was lying.

But why?

Ever so gently, he touched her cheek with his thumb. "Have you been crying?"

She couldn't bear to look at him. "A little."

"You'll be back with Noah in two days."

"I know." She cleared her throat and forced herself to look straight at Jack. He was dressed in jeans and a blue-and-white striped shirt. "Are we leaving for the shipyard soon?"

"About thirty minutes. I'm going to have some breakfast first. What about you?"

"I'm not hungry. I'll change into something more businesslike and join you back here in half an hour."

"Dress casually," he said.

Kyra started to walk past him, but Jack gently caught her arm. "Is what happened between us last night upsetting you?"

Kyra turned her head and looked into his eyes. "Yes." Her voice wasn't much more than a whisper.

"Why?"

"Because we have a professional relationship. It shouldn't have happened. I shouldn't have allowed myself to—"

"Get so out of control?" Jack finished for her. "I lost control, too. Neither of us could have stopped. I wanted you." He gazed lingeringly at her lovely face. "I still want you. I think I have from the moment you walked into my office. You make me feel…"

Jack shook his head.

"That's it. You make me feel. I look at you—touch

you—and I discover emotions I didn't know I was capable of.''

Kyra's eyes filled with tears.

Jack reached up and wiped the warm saltiness from her cheek. ''More tears?''

''It wasn't supposed to happen like this.''

Without caring who might have been in the lobby, Jack pulled her into his arms and held her close, his lips against her hair. ''Last night was as natural for both of us as breathing. It was inevitable. You know it and I know it.''

He was right. Kyra had to admit it. What she'd felt about this man last night—what she still felt about him this morning—had nothing to do with her work. Her response to him was absolute and pure.

''Neither of us has anything to be ashamed of or to apologize for,'' Jack said.

Kyra pulled away and looked up at him. ''I need time.''

''For what?''

''To figure out what it is I'm feeling.''

He turned Kyra to face him completely, his hands resting on her shoulders. ''Don't regret it, Kyra. I don't.''

She could feel her throat start to close.

''When you want to talk, let me know.''

She nodded.

Jack reluctantly let her go and watched as she walked away from him. She looked so sad that he wanted to pull her back into his arms. For a moment he almost forgot...

But not quite.

There was something else.

He turned toward the telephone and stared at it.

Who had she called?

Jack turned to a man who was standing nearby. "Excuse me," he said, "but would you do me a favor and watch this phone for a minute until I get back? Don't let anyone use it."

The man looked a little confused, but shrugged his shoulders in agreement.

Jack walked to the front desk. The woman behind it lit up as he approached.

"Mr. Allessandro! How are you this morning?"

"Fine," he said absently. "I want a number traced."

She suddenly looked as though she were out of her league.

"Get the manager," he ordered.

The woman left and returned with another woman. "Yes, sir. What can I do for you?"

Jack pointed to the pay phone still guarded by the stranger. "A call was just made from that phone. Probably long distance. I want you to find out the number that was called."

"Right away."

The woman looked something up in her phone book and pressed the number. In Spanish, she explained what hotel she was with and what she needed. Then she looked up the number of the pay phone and gave it to the person on the other end of the line.

Placing her hand over the mouthpiece of the receiver, she whispered, "Isn't it amazing what telephone companies can do these days?"

Jack didn't say anything.

They waited for more than five minutes.

Then the manager responded to something being said to her and scribbled a number on her pad. Hanging up the phone, she ripped the small sheet of paper off the pad and handed it to him. "He didn't know the name of the party being called, but he said it was a Washington, D.C., area code."

"Thank you," Jack said.

He looked at the number a long moment. Whoever Kyra had been talking to, it certainly hadn't been Noah and her aunt.

Why would she lie?

And why would she be calling Washington?

He didn't feel good about this. He'd learned a long time ago to trust his gut.

And his gut told him that something was going on.

The key for the moment was to behave the same as he had been.

It wouldn't be hard.

He truly had feelings for Kyra.

And he hoped with all his heart that she didn't have any dark secrets.

Chapter 11

As Kyra walked to the helicopter, she saw Jack standing beside it, waiting for her.

Her heart leaped. She couldn't help it.

And it showed in her eyes for the world—and Jack—to see.

Taking her face in both of his hands, Jack kissed her with a tenderness that made her ache.

But this was the path to disaster.

Kyra put her hands over his. "Don't please."

"Why not?"

"Because I can't think rationally when you touch me."

The grooves in his cheeks deepened. "That's a bad thing?"

"A very bad thing. I have a lot to consider, not the least of which is my son."

"I would never do anything to hurt Noah."

"Not intentionally. But I have to be very careful about any romantic involvements."

"And?"

Kyra rubbed her forehead. "I wish I could take last night back. I wish it had never happened."

"Why?" he asked quietly.

"Nothing between us can ever be the same. Everything has changed."

"Making love with a person tends to do that."

"Jack, I work for you. Do you know how awkward this is going to be for both of us?"

"It doesn't have to be. You're making it that way."

"I don't want to be having an affair with my boss."

"Are you ready?" the pilot yelled out at them.

The two of them looked at each other for a long moment. Then Jack took Kyra's arm and silently helped her into the helicopter.

"I'm sorry," said Kyra over her shoulder.

"Don't apologize for being honest," Jack said.

She slid onto the bench seat and buckled herself in. Jack sat beside her and did the same, then signaled the pilot that they were ready.

The helicopter rose straight into the air and then swooped toward Barcelona.

Kyra stared out the window.

Jack leaned over and spoke in her ear. It was the only way short of shouting that she could hear him. "I know there's more. Go ahead and say what you need to."

Kyra continued looking outside for a moment, then turned toward Jack as far as her seat belt would allow and took his hand in both of hers. It was a strong hand, and yet capable of such gentleness when it came to touching her.

She raised his hand to her cheek and held it there. "What happened last night can never happen again."

"You mean you don't want it to."

Kyra nodded.

"Why?"

"I don't want..." She cleared her throat as he put his hand on his own lap and released it. "I can't have that kind of relationship with you."

"Because I'm your boss?"

"That's part of it."

"Then stop working for me. Let me support you and Noah."

"After one night together, you'd do that?"

There was no hesitation. "Yes."

"I can't let you. It wouldn't be right. I'm used to fending for myself and Noah. That's the way it's always been."

"So where do we go from here?"

"I want things to go back to the way they were."

Despite what he was feeling, Jack's expression didn't change. "Do you think they can?"

"They have to." Kyra shook her head. "Look, I don't have affairs—at least I didn't until last night—and I don't envision myself as anyone's mistress. I just want to be able to do my job without last night haunting me."

Jack was in an awkward position. He wanted Kyra and he knew that feeling wasn't going to change. But he was also her boss. He had a responsibility to Kyra beyond his personal feelings. If she was uncomfortable with their relationship, he had to allow her to back away and give her whatever distance she needed for however long she needed it.

"All right," he said.

Kyra looked at him in surprise. "Just like that?"

"Just like that."

Kyra couldn't begin to describe her relief. Her smile transformed her face. "Thank you."

What Kyra didn't know was just how eloquent her expression was when she looked at him. It told him things she had no idea she was saying.

He knew that Kyra was in love with him.

And he knew she wasn't being honest with him.

There were a lot of questions that needed answering, but he would wait for as long as it took her to come around—and for him to find out what was really going on behind those eyes.

The rest of the trip was accomplished in a surprisingly comfortable silence. When they landed, Jack got out first and looked straight into Kyra's eyes as he put his hands on her waist and lowered her to the ground. Then he guided her away from the helicopter's whirling blades to the car that would drive them to the docks.

"These belong to the company," Jack said, pointing to a series of huge warehouses as they approached their destination. "We warehouse shipments here both before they're loaded and after they're unloaded."

"I imagine you have to have good security."

"We've had some theft, but not that much."

"Do you use video?"

"Of course."

"And someone to monitor the cameras?"

"Yes."

"Motion detectors?"

"That wouldn't be possible. There's always someone coming in and going out."

"What about individual shipments? Are they wired so that they can't be moved without detection?"

"No." Jack turned to look at her. "Why are you so interested in security?"

"It was very important at the last company I was with. I just wondered if you took some of the same precautions."

He continued looking at her.

Kyra began to wonder if she'd been convincing enough in her answer.

"I see," he finally said.

The car stopped on the dock, between the sea and the warehouses. As Jack climbed out of the car, a man walked over to him carrying two red hard hats. As Jack gave Kyra a hand out of the car, he handed her a hat. "Put this on."

A freighter was being unloaded just as they arrived. Men were shouting back and forth as the machinery used to lift and haul the load roared. The huge hook of a crane swung over her head toward the freighter. Kyra watched as a man on the deck of the freighter grabbed the hook and attached it to the rope rigging of a semitrailer. Then he got out of the way and within moments the trailer was airborne.

It swung out over the dock and was precisely maneuvered into a neat row with a dozen others just like it.

Then the process began all over again.

It was a warm day with the sun reflecting brightly

off the water as they walked. There was an interesting
smell in the air—a combination of machinery, salt-
water, petroleum and sweat.

Kyra watched and listened as Jack walked along
the docks, talking to the men—and the occasional
woman. She heard him asking about their families,
their lives, if there were any problems he needed to
know about.

The dock workers seemed to know and like Jack,
if their enthusiasm when they shook his hand was any
indication.

Barry, looking the worse for wear but sporting different clothes than he'd had on the night before,
caught up to them.

He put his hand in the middle of Kyra's back as
they walked. "See anything interesting?"

"Everything, but then I've never been on a dock
before."

"Noisy, isn't it?"

"More than I imagined." She looked at him sideways. "How was your evening?"

He grinned. "Long, but extremely pleasant. You
look a little tired yourself. Late night?"

"Jet lag." Kyra changed the subject. "Is coming
to the docks part of your usual routine?"

"No. That's Jack's end of the business."

"So why are you here?"

"I think it's time for me to take a more active role
in the business side of things."

"Why?"

"My name goes on everything, just like Jack's. I
think it's time I paid attention to what I'm signing."

"What's changed to make you feel that way?"

Barry shrugged. "Maybe I'm growing up."

Kyra lifted an eyebrow.

"Hey, better late than never, right?"

"Are you going to incorporate that into your private life?"

"What can I say? I've never been able to resist a beautiful woman. I don't see that changing any time soon."

They had fallen several yards behind Jack, but Kyra was still watching him. Her interest was piqued when she saw him silently signal a dock worker on one of the oil tankers.

The worker returned the gesture with a nearly imperceptible nod.

"Who's that man on the tanker?"

Barry looked up. "Which one?"

"The tall one in the navy blue T-shirt."

Barry squinted into the sunlight. "I don't know. I've never seen him before. Why?"

"Just curious."

"He might be one of our employees. I can't tell the regular dock workers from our guys."

"Jack seems to know everyone by name."

"I know. I guess he's trying to show he's still one of the guys."

"Still?"

"He worked on the docks while he was putting himself through school."

"I didn't know that." Kyra couldn't believe that bit of information hadn't been in Riley's file on Jack.

"That's when he first got interested in owning his own shipping company."

"It's amazing that he's been able to accomplish as

much as he has. It's a long trip from dock worker to shipping magnate.''

"Not as long as it looks.''

"What's that mean?''

"It's a business full of corruption on both sides of the desk. If you're smart and keep your eyes and ears open, anything is possible.''

"Are you suggesting that Jack is corrupt?''

"Jack has always done what needed to be done to take care of his family. No one can fault the man for that. Sometimes the difference between right and wrong isn't white or black, but a shady area. If you maneuver through it carefully enough, the rewards can be tremendous.''

"Everyone gets caught eventually.''

Barry smiled at her as though she were a naive child. "What planet are you living on, Kyra? People get away with murder, never mind a few corrupt business practices. Don't you read the papers?''

"Apparently not the same ones you do.''

"When it suits the government's purpose—be it America, Spain or anywhere between—if it benefits them to look the other way, that's exactly what they do.''

"Interesting theory.''

"It's more than a theory, Kyra.''

"Does Franco agree with you?''

Barry looked at her in surprise. "Why do you ask?''

"You seemed to agree on a lot of things at dinner last night.''

Barry nodded. "Yeah, well, Franco and I have a lot in common.''

"That surprises me."

"It happens that I like the man. In fact, I wish we were doing business with him instead of his father. He knows how I feel."

"What about Jack?"

He shrugged. "Jack plays his cards pretty close to the vest. I never know what he's thinking. When I've tried to guess, I've been wrong. But I'll tell you one thing. Jack's a practical guy. He'll work with whomever pulls the financial strings in the Zamora family. The thing is," explained Barry, "Franco understands how things are done in today's world. He's ready to move forward. His old man's stuck in the past."

"I expect Franco will be taking over the business in the not too distant future when his father retires."

Barry laughed, but he didn't look amused. "That's not going to happen. Jose will hang on to his power until his last gasp."

"How do you know that?"

"I know the type." He inclined his head toward his partner. "Jack's a lot like him."

"In what way?"

"He has one way of doing things—his way. He won't deviate, even if a better way comes along."

"Doing things his way has made you both a lot of money."

"Yeah, well, sometimes it isn't as much the money as it is the game."

"What game?"

"You know. The game. Outsmarting the other guy."

"And that's important to you?"

"Me and every other man in the business world.

That's the whole challenge of business, Kyra. What else is there if you're not out to win and win big?''

"Interesting philosophy."

As they walked, he pointed out a tanker freighter. "That's one of the tankers we use for Zamora."

Kyra was genuinely in awe. "It's huge."

"That's the word."

Jack walked back to them at that moment. "Glad you made it, Barry."

Barry nodded.

"We were just talking about how big the tankers are," said Kyra.

"Too big," said Jack as he looked at the tanker.

Kyra shielded her eyes from the sun as her gaze swept the tanker from one end to the other. "Too big for what?" she asked.

"They're fine for the trip to Barcelona with a full load, but then we send them back to the Middle East empty for the next load. We should be able to haul freight in both directions. It would save us a lot of money."

"I think you're worrying too much about that," said Barry. "I think we should do business as usual with Zamora now and work on getting the tanker loaded for a return trip later."

"And if we don't get a return load?" Both Jack's look and tone were surprisingly pointed.

"Then we still make money. Just not as much."

"Heads up!" shouted a worker as a huge box swung out over them.

Jack took Kyra by the elbow and steered her toward one of the buildings. "Have you seen enough to give you a general idea of what the docks are like?'' he asked.

''Yes.''

''Then go back to the hotel. We were supposed to have a dinner tonight, but something has come up and I'm going to cancel. You have the evening free to do whatever you want. We'll leave for Chicago tomorrow afternoon.''

Kyra wanted to stay on the docks so she could watch what was going on. ''Since you're going to be tied up here for several hours, would you mind if I just wandered around on my own?''

''Why would you want to do that?'' asked Jack.

''So I can learn more about the company. Besides, I've never been on a dock before. It's interesting.''

''This is no place for a novice to be wandering around. If you don't know what you're doing, you can get hurt.''

''I'll be fine. Really. I'll make sure I'm not any place dangerous. I can even stay with you.''

''No. You can wander around Barcelona if you want, but not around here.''

Kyra didn't argue. ''All right.'' She tried not to sound too disappointed.

''You can take the driver. When you're finished in the city, go ahead and take the car back to the hotel.''

''What about you?''

''I'll take the helicopter.''

''All right.''

''Do you need me for anything?'' asked Barry.

''I'm going to meet with the dock supervisor and warehouse manager in about an hour. You can stick around for that if you want.''

"Pass."

Kyra looked at Barry in surprise. "I thought you wanted to get more involved in the business end of things."

"I do, but there's no need to become obsessive."

Kyra rolled her eyes.

"Where do you have meetings?" Kyra asked, looking around. "Right on the docks?"

"We have offices inside the third warehouse," said Jack. "Barry, take the helicopter and send it back for me. Just make sure you're at the airport on time tomorrow."

"You know," said Kyra, "if you're going to have a meeting, you might need me to take notes." She wanted in on that meeting.

"It's not necessary. Nothing monumental is going to be said."

"But—"

"Goodbye, Kyra," Jack said as he turned away from her. "Just enjoy the rest of the day. I'll see you tomorrow."

Kyra watched Jack walk away from them. She couldn't take her eyes off his broad shoulders.

"You look like a disappointed puppy," Barry said as he put his hand under her elbow and turned her around. "You couldn't possibly want to stick around here to sit through some boring meetings that badly."

"I enjoy my job."

"A little too much, if you ask me," said Barry. "It's not natural."

"I've always liked working," she said casually as they walked toward the car.

"Each to his own." Barry opened the car door for

her and climbed in after her. ''Helicopter,'' he said to the driver as he sank back into his seat. ''Ever been to Barcelona?''

''Many times.''

''You like it?''

''Very much.''

As they arrived at the helicopter, Barry opened the door and stepped out. ''See you tomorrow, kid.''

Kyra settled back into her seat as the car drove off. If Jack thought for one minute he was going to get rid of her that easily, he was mistaken. If the meeting was supposed to be about nothing, he would have let her stay. This meeting was definitely about something.

And she was going to be there.

And Jack would be none the wiser.

Chapter 12

The drive to the city was a short one. Kyra stared out the darkly tinted window of the car, oblivious to the architecturally ornate buildings that comprised some of the most spectacular cathedrals in the world.

She pressed the speaker button to get the driver's attention.

"Ma'am?"

"Drop me off in front of the hotel one block ahead on the right."

"Yes, ma'am."

"You can have the next four hours to do whatever you want. I'll meet you back at the hotel at six o'clock."

He nodded his head as he pulled to the curb and got out of the car to open the door for her.

"Thank you."

"Six o'clock," he repeated.

"Yes."

"I'll be here."

"If I'm a little late, please wait for me."

"Of course."

Kyra stood on the sidewalk and watched the driver get back into the car and pull into the flow of traffic.

When he was out of sight, she walked through the gold-framed revolving door of the Hotel de Barcelona—a hotel she was familiar with from having stayed there years earlier. She walked through the lobby to an empty meeting room as though she belonged there.

She closed the large double doors behind her, pulled one of the carved-back, red-cushioned chairs out of the way so she could sit on the round mahogany table, pulled out her cellular phone and pressed Riley's office number. He answered on the second ring.

"Riley, it's me."

"If this is what we talked about earlier—"

"It isn't."

"Then go ahead."

"I'm in Barcelona. I just left the docks used by Allessandro Shipping. Jack stayed behind for a meeting he didn't want me to attend. I'm going back there to look around and to see what I can overhear."

"Is it safe?"

"I don't know. People saw me around there earlier, so perhaps they won't think anything of me hanging around now."

"Let's hope not."

"What I need to know from you is what I should look for while I'm there."

"What are the facilities like?"

"Several huge warehouses with offices in one of them. A wide dock area where the cargo is unloaded and some of it stored right on the docks. There are also several freighters and tankers moored there at the moment."

"Okay. Any way to get onto the freighters?"

"Not during daylight."

"Then stick to the warehouses. Listen to conversations among the workers and do your best not to look conspicuous."

"Thanks for the insights," said Kyra dryly.

"Don't be sarcastic. How long do you expect this little adventure to take?"

"I'm not sure. I told the limo driver to pick me up at six o'clock Barcelona time to drive me back to Costa Azul."

"I want to hear from you the minute you're clear of the docks."

"I'll call."

"How are you getting to the docks?"

"Renting a car."

"That's good."

"Gotta go now."

"Okay. And Kyra? Be careful. Noah needs his mother."

"You should have thought of that before you assigned me to this case."

"You're an investigator. You can't pick and choose your cases any more than anyone else who works for the DOJ."

"I know." Her tone was somewhat apologetic. "I'll be careful."

"Good girl. Call me."

Kyra slipped the phone into her purse, slid off the table and walked through the lobby of the hotel and back to the street. Two doors down was a car rental agency. Using her passport and Virginia driver's license as identification, she rented a dark compact car.

The agency sent her in one of their vans to a car park several blocks away and dropped her off next to her rental. Climbing into the driver's seat, she checked everything out before starting the engine and backing out of the space.

Getting to the docks would be easy, but getting out of the city in the traffic at this hour would be more difficult. But she persevered, moving at a snail's pace until she hit the open highway.

She parked the rental in the lot with cars of the dock workers and just sat there for a moment, looking around.

It was a busy place.

People were coming and going constantly.

Taking a deep breath, she climbed out of the car, closed the door, shouldered her purse and headed for the warehouses, hands casually in her trouser pockets and looking as though she hadn't a care in the world.

Some of the men who'd seen her earlier smiled and inclined their heads. Kyra smiled back. The ones who didn't know she'd been with their boss stared at her with intense appreciation.

She went to the warehouse where Jack had said the offices were and walked in through the open doors. If she ran into Jack, she would have to think of something to say, but at the moment she didn't have a clue what it would be.

The warehouse seemed even larger from the inside, and crates with painted labels packed it from floor to ceiling. She strolled among them, checking out their places of departure, destinations and contents. She didn't see anything there from the United States.

Her sleeve caught on the corner of one of the crates and tore it slightly. "Damn," she whispered as she backed up to disengage the material from the rough wood. It was one of her favorite shirts.

Kyra leaned against the crate as she carefully worked the material away from the splinters. She was focused on the splinter, but her attention was suddenly grabbed by an obscured label behind the paint that currently read *Canada*. Forgetting about her shirt, Kyra leaned in closer. It was very faint, but she could make out portions of some of the letters, and they seemed to spell out *United States of America*.

Hmm.

So they had relabeled the crates to change the country of origin.

Kyra retraced her steps, examining the painted labels on different crates. The one she'd gotten caught on was the only one that had been altered. All of the others had either been done more carefully or hadn't been changed in the first place. She couldn't tell which.

If she had to guess, Kyra would say that they'd probably been changed.

Why? she asked herself.

So their points of origin would be disguised.

And why do that?

Because crates of scrap from Canada would never raise suspicions. It made perfect sense. Shipping government scrap from the United States to Canada wouldn't raise any eyebrows. The crates heading for China and Iran were the ones that got searched most often. Once in Canada, they probably changed the country of origin on the crates and sent them to Barcelona. From here they would be sent to China and Iran. It increased the paperwork and made the trail harder to follow.

Not too shabby.

Kyra stared at the crate. Her emotions were mixed. She'd found something important and she knew it.

She just didn't want Jack to be involved.

She moved through the crates, more careful with her clothes this time.

It must have been afternoon break time because the warehouse was silent and deserted. The outside noise, which was considerably less than it had been earlier, seemed distant and muffled. Kyra could hear the rustle of her own clothes, the deliberate softness of each footfall.

She moved carefully, on the alert for any movement or noise, staying as close to the wall as she could until she reached the end of the crate storage area and could go no farther. She was now a good fifteen feet from the office.

Kyra knelt behind a crate while she studied the office. The front wall was entirely glass and stretched for perhaps fifteen feet. A narrow hallway ran parallel to the solid right wall of the office, off of which were the rest rooms. They were probably for the office workers rather than the dock workers.

Kyra craned her neck to see inside. A lone man—the one from the docks she'd noticed Jack talk-

ing to earlier   sat behind a desk talking on the phone.
A woman was at another desk, typing on a computer
keyboard.

Kyra couldn't get from where she was to where the
office was without putting herself clearly in their line
of sight.

Suddenly the woman pulled a sheaf of papers out
of the printer and walked to the man's desk with
them. The woman's back was to Kyra and she was
blocking the windows from the man's view.

Kyra didn't think twice. Keeping her body bent
low, she raced across the open area to the narrow hall.
She saw as soon as she was there that she'd been
mistaken about a solid wall. It was glass from about
four feet from the floor to the ceiling.

And there was a door.

Kyra straightened a little so she could see into the
office. The woman was back at her computer. The
man was still at his desk.

She made a quick survey of the area inside the
office closest to her. There were boxes on either side
of the door. She would easily be able to hide behind
them. The problem was that if anyone left the office
to use the rest rooms, they would be able to see her
quite clearly.

It was a chance she would have to take.

Still bent low, Kyra went to the door and quietly
pressed down on the handle.

It was locked. Damn. Now what was she supposed
to do?

She heard footsteps on the concrete of the warehouse floor coming toward the office and low voices
speaking in Spanish. She moved away from the door

and peered above the glass again so she could see what was going on.

Several men came into view.

One was Jack. That was fine—he was supposed to be there.

And then her heart sank. It was becoming an unpleasantly familiar sensation.

With him were Franco Zamora and Burton Banacomp.

Oh, Jack, she thought. What on earth are you doing with those men?

It was becoming an unpleasantly familiar question.

The men entered the office. Jack said something to the woman and she stopped working, collected her purse and left the office, closing the door behind her.

While the men were involved in greeting one another, Kyra quietly tried to find a place where she could hear what was going on. The most likely spot appeared to be the door.

Pressing her ear against the one-eighth-inch breech in the door closure, she took a soft breath and held it.

Nothing.

Stretching her neck slightly she peered through the glass. Jack and Franco sat across from the man behind the desk. Their lips were moving.

She pressed her ear against the breech again.

She could hear the low hum of voices, but no clear words.

She pressed her ear closer. Mumble, mumble, mumble, and then... "...changed in Canada, and I've given them new inventory numbers and destinations."

Kyra didn't recognize the voice. More conversation followed that she couldn't hear clearly, but she picked up scattered phrases. "Two days. Different freighter than before…"

The noise from an air vent about ten feet away suddenly stopped and she could hear Franco's voice clearly.

"I'm glad Barry's out of the picture. He made me nervous. The man is as unreliable as they come." Franco laughed. "I wish I could have seen his face last night when he came to the warehouse expecting to find crates from the U.S. and they were nowhere to be found. How do you suppose he's going to explain the missing—" he paused "—scrap?"

"Not my problem," Jack said.

"That's cold," said Franco. "What are you going to do if he finds out you've done an end run around him in our dealings with the congressman and China?"

"He won't."

"Said like a true Allessandro," said Franco.

Jack must have said something she missed because the next moment Franco was apologizing.

"Sorry. You know I meant it as a compliment. As for me, I'm not going to apologize for what I'm doing. I'm sick and tired of living under my father's thumb. This is my chance to break away and show the world what I can do on my own."

"The only way the world will ever know about it is if you get caught," Jack said.

"True. On the other hand, another year of this and I'll have the money to bump my father out of the business and run it the way I think it should be run.

That'll be my statement to the world. We all know why the congressman is doing it: the money. Why are you doing it, Jack? It can't be for the money.''

Silence.

''Perhaps it's because you're bored. This is your way of putting a little excitement back into your life.''

''My reasons for doing anything are none of your business,'' said Jack, ''so stop psychoanalyzing me and get on with it.''

The fan kicked on again and the words were drowned out.

Kyra was numb. She stopped trying to listen and leaned her forehead against the wood of the door frame.

Jack was in it up to his neck.

Her Jack.

She felt an uncontrollable nausea rising. Her elbow hit the door as she raised her hand to her mouth and bent double.

Four pairs of eyes turned in the direction of the thud.

Kyra froze, bile in her throat. They had to have heard that.

She had to get out of there—fast.

But how? Glass was all around.

She moved along the wall away from the door and carefully peeked inside. Jack and Franco were on their feet and heading in her direction.

Looking frantically around, the only place she could see to go was the rest room, but they would see the door open.

Still crouched, she moved quickly to the bathroom, pushed the door open, then turned as though she was on her way out and emptied the contents of her purse—except for her phone—onto the floor.

When Jack and Franco came out of the office and found her, she was on her knees in the doorway of the rest room putting things back into her purse. She looked up at them with what she hoped was a chagrined smile. "This is the second time I've done this today," she said as she dropped her lipstick back into her bag and rose. "I think I should have stayed in bed this morning."

Neither man smiled. "What are you doing here?" asked Franco.

"I asked her to come," Jack said before she could answer, then stepped in front of her, raised her face to his with a finger under her chin and lightly kissed her on the lips. "You're late, darling."

"Sorry," she said, following his lead. "I got lost."

"Wait for me in front of the warehouse," he said.

Kyra didn't have to be asked twice. She wanted to run, but forced herself to walk calmly past the window where Burton Banacomp and the other man watched with narrowed eyes.

"What the hell is she doing here?" asked the congressman as Franco and Jack reentered the office.

"She came to meet me," said Jack. "Nothing sinister."

"What was she doing outside the office?"

"Using the rest room."

"What if she overheard something?" asked Franco.

"She couldn't have," said Jack. "But even if she did, so what? She's in love with me. She's not going to rock the boat."

"I don't like it," said Franco. "I told you before what the rumors are about her."

"What rumors?" asked Banacomp.

"That she works for the government," said Franco.

"She works for me," Jack said sharply. "I've had her checked out from one end to the other. There's no way she works for any arm of the government. Her life is an open book."

"I don't like it," said Banacomp. "No one but you three were supposed to know I was here. Now she's seen me."

"You're here to promote trade between Spain and the U.S. Touring the docks are part and parcel of that," said Jack. "Kyra isn't going to make anything of that. Neither will anyone else unless you make an issue of it."

"We're all at risk here," said Franco. "Even more so with her around. I'm going to have her checked out myself, and if I'm not satisfied with what I find out, she's history."

The muscle in Jack's jaw moved, but other than that, he was completely calm, a tactic his opponents usually found more frightening than overt anger. He stood in front of Franco, face-to-face. "If you so much as look in Kyra's direction, I'll take you out so fast you'll think you were hit by lightning." His voice was as cold and smooth as steel. "Do you understand?"

Franco knew when to back down.

"Do you understand?" Jack repeated.

"Yeah," Franco said.

Then Jack turned to look at the others. "Anyone else have a problem they want to discuss with me?"

The man behind the desk held up his hand. "No, man. I'm clear."

"Let's do it," said Banacomp.

Kyra had gone to the front of the warehouse, but she stood behind a stack of crates as she pulled out her telephone and called Riley.

He answered on the first ring.

"Thank God," she said when she heard his voice.

"Kyra? Are you all right?"

"Just listen. I don't have much time. You need to get some men to the Allessandro warehouse in Barcelona as soon as possible. There are some crates with Canadian points of origin that have our scrap in them. They're going to be heading for China. Banacomp is here and in it up to his neck, along with Franco Zamora and another man who works here whose name I don't know."

"And Jack?"

Kyra took a long breath. "Jack, too."

"I'm sorry, Kyra."

"What do you want me to do now?"

"Just get yourself home. Your part in this is finished. We'll take it from here."

"Riley?"

"Yeah."

"Jack just helped me out of a tight spot. Whatever happens, please make sure he doesn't get hurt."

"We'll do our best."

"I know. Thanks."

As soon as she disconnected, she walked to the edge of the dock. Standing beside one of the freighters as though she was enjoying the view, she let the phone slip from her fingers. It disappeared into the murky water with a plunk.

She stood there a moment longer, then went back into the warehouse and sat on a crate to wait.

She still felt ill.

Heartsick.

And a little nervous. Jack had lied for her, which meant he didn't believe for a moment that she'd been in the rest room.

That left her with two questions. The first one was, why had he come to her rescue? The second one was, what was he thinking?

She heard the men's footsteps on the concrete floor as they approached her. Kyra remained on the crates, swinging her feet back and forth, behaving as casually as she could.

Franco walked straight toward her and, without a word, picked up her purse and emptied its contents onto a crate. Poking through the lipstick, hairbrush, pens, keys and hair scrunchies, he looked at her sideways. "That's it?"

"What else were you expecting?" she asked.

He looked at her for a long moment, then walked away.

Kyra tried to look more annoyed than frightened as she gathered her things and put them back. "What was that all about?" she asked Jack.

"Suppose you tell me," he said.

"Tell you what?"

"What you were really doing near the office?"

Kyra didn't let her expression change at all. "I finished sightseeing early. Unfortunately I'd instructed your driver not to pick me up until later this afternoon. I was bored, so I rented a car and came back here to find you."

"And so you have." His gaze was unwavering. "How long were you inside the warehouse before we found you?"

"Ages. I wasn't feeling very well. I'd been in the rest room for quite a while and when I came out, you were there. I apologize if I interrupted anything."

Jack's expression didn't change. Kyra couldn't tell whether he believed her or not. "Have you finished your business?" she asked.

Taking her elbow firmly in his hand, Jack turned her around and walked her out of the warehouse and around to the parking lot. "Which one is yours?"

She pointed to the dark compact.

"Give me the keys."

She opened her purse, fumbled through her things for a moment before finally locating them, then put them in his outstretched hand.

"Get in," he told her as he walked around to the driver's side.

Jack was clearly angry, and she was suddenly frightened. "What's wrong?"

"Just get in!"

"Where are we going?" she asked as she fastened her seat belt and he started the engine.

He was silent.

"I have to return the car to Barcelona."

"It'll be taken care of."

"The helicopter—"

"Can find its way back to the hotel without me."

Kyra sat straight in her seat. Her hand hovered over the door handle. Should she just jump out and make a run for it?

Chapter 13

She decided against escaping and remained in the car. A situation hadn't arisen yet that she couldn't talk her way out of. This one was no different.

The problem was not knowing exactly what the "situation" was.

Jack drove fast, and he didn't say another word. To her relief, he pulled up in front of the hotel. Tossing the keys to the parking attendant, he walked around the car to open her door, then held her arm so tightly it hurt as he escorted her into the hotel to the elevator.

Upon reaching their private suite, Jack shoved her into a chair and stood towering over her. "I want to know what the hell is going on," he said.

Kyra looked at him in bewilderment. "I told you—"

"My two-year-old niece could come up with a better story than that." He leaned toward her, his hands on either armrest, his face inches from hers. "Who are you?"

Kyra's heart was hammering so loudly in her ears that everything else faded into background noise except Jack's voice. "I'm Kyra Courtland. You know my whole history. Check—"

"I have checked. The name is right. The pedigree is right. The work history is perfect. But the timing is interesting. How convenient that you, with your remarkable credentials, showed up at just the moment my other assistant had to leave."

"Talk to my last employer. He'll tell you—"

"Tell me what? That you were a good and loyal employee?"

"Yes."

Jack straightened away from her, anger in every line of his body. "Do you have any idea how close you came to ruining everything?" he asked.

"Ruining what?"

He didn't hear her question. "I don't know what your game is, Kyra. I do know that everything you've said since we met—everything you've done—has been a lie."

"Everything *I've* said? Everything *I've* done?"

"Who are you really working for?" he asked. "Was Franco right? Are you with the government?"

"I'm your assistant! I don't understand what all the excitement is about. You've asked me to sit in on your meetings in the past. Today I'm in a room ten feet from where you're having a meeting, with two walls between us, and suddenly I'm doing something wrong."

"You were supposed to be ten miles from the docks."

"I told you already. I got bored."

"Well, now we have a problem."

"Why?"

Jack knelt in front of her so they were eye level. "Kyra, I need for you to be honest with me. This is life and death. Is there anything you're not telling me? Anything I should know?"

He looked so sincere. He made her want to tell him who she really was.

"Tell me, Kyra. There's too much at stake for lies now."

The conversation she overheard at the warehouse played over and over in her mind. "I don't know what you want me to say. I am who I am."

Jack looked deeply into her eyes, searching her soul for the truth. In that moment, he knew Franco had been right. "You're a very poor liar, Kyra."

"I don't have to listen to this," she said as she started to rise.

"Sit down," he ordered in a voice that shook the walls.

She did.

"Don't move."

Kyra watched as he went into the office, leaving the door open so he could see her. He picked up the phone and spoke to the person on the other end for several minutes. Kyra couldn't hear what was being said, but she heard Jack angrily raise his voice.

When he returned, he stood over her. "I'm having Noah and your aunt picked up and taken to a safe place."

Kyra's heart flew into her throat "What?"

"What happened today put both you and your family in danger."

Kyra flew out of her chair and straight at Jack, hands fisted. She rammed him so hard it knocked him off balance and they both fell to the floor. He caught her hand before she could reach his face and managed to flip her onto her back, pinning her arms high over her head with his hands and holding her struggling body down with his.

"Calm down," he said.

She only struggled harder.

"Kyra, your family is fine."

"If you do anything to them, so help me I'll hunt you down and—"

"Kyra, look at me."

"Let go!"

Jack adjusted himself so that his body pressed hers more securely to the floor. "Look at me. Look into my eyes."

Kyra couldn't move. The struggle was getting her nowhere. With eyes full of resentment, she turned her head and glared at him.

"I would never do anything to hurt your family."

"How do I know that?"

"Because I'm telling you so. I'm having them moved to protect them. That's the only reason."

"Protect them from whom?"

"Franco, for one. He thinks you're working for the government and he's going to check it out. If he discovers his hunch is correct, no one in your family will be safe."

Kyra's body went limp.

"If I let go of you now, will you behave?"

"Yes."

He let go of her wrists and did a push-up with his hands on either side of her head to lift his body from hers, then gave her a hand up.

"Do you feel like telling me the truth now?"

It went against everything she'd ever been taught. Never let anyone know who you worked for. But this involved her family.

She sat in the chair. "I'm with the Department of Justice."

"And why is the Department of Justice interested in me?"

"They think you're involved in smuggling our technology to foreign powers who are less than friendly toward the United States."

"Why focus on me?"

"You know all the principals. Information coming out of your corporation suggests that you're personally involved."

He knew there was more. "And?"

She looked up at him. "And I overheard you today. I know the truth."

"You know what you heard, which just might have very little bearing on the truth."

"Don't play word games with me."

Jack reached out to touch her cheek, but Kyra jerked away. "What happens now?"

Jack walked away from her to the window and stared outside. "You stay with me for the next twenty-four hours. After that, you can join your family."

Kyra didn't trust what he was saying. "Why would you let me go, knowing what I know about you?"

He turned to look at her. "What do you suggest I do, Kyra? Throw you into the ocean?"

"That seems the more logical solution. I'm sure your grandfather wouldn't have hesitated to do that."

"Ah," said Jack. "My grandfather. Everything in my life eventually goes back to him. You think that because I'm the grandson of Tony Allessandro I must be like him."

"I didn't," she said quietly. "I truly didn't until a few hours ago."

"One conversation was all it took to convince you."

"I'd say it was a fairly defining moment."

His expression didn't change, but Kyra knew something inside him had. "Then there's nothing more to say." He looked at his watch. "It would appear that the two of us are going to be joined at the hip for the next twenty-four hours," he said matter-of-factly. "Get used to it. I don't want you talking to anyone or making any phone calls."

"Not even to Noah or my aunt?"

"There's no need. You'll see them tomorrow."

"What happens if I choose not to do as I'm told?"

"You could get us both killed."

She looked into his eyes for a long moment and didn't doubt a word he said.

"Go to your room, Kyra. Pack your clothes. Get some sleep."

She rose from the chair and walked away from him, aware that his gaze followed her.

Closing the door behind her with a soft click, Kyra

sank onto the bed. She'd told Riley all she could before dumping her phone. Even now she didn't know anything more she could have passed along even if she'd had access to a telephone.

And she didn't know that she would have made a call if she could.

She sat there for a long time, not bothering to turn on the lights in her room, trying to put things in a logical frame. Was Jack a bad guy or not? She knew what she'd heard. But if he were bad, why would he have protected her when she was caught in the warehouse?

And if he weren't why was he involved with those men at all?

There didn't seem to be any middle ground. He had to be a bad guy.

And yet she trusted him—completely and without hesitation—to take care of Noah and Emily, and keep them safe.

Nor did she think he would do anything to harm her.

Safe in the arms of the enemy. Who would have thought?

Crossing the dark room, Kyra opened her sliding-glass door and stepped onto the veranda. Jack was there, standing at the point where his room connected to Barry's, his hands on the railing, staring out into the starlit darkness.

Jack didn't turn his head. He didn't have to. He knew exactly where she was. "Need some fresh air?" he asked.

"Yes. You, too, I gather." She stood beside him,

her arm touching his as she leaned on the railing. "I've been trying to figure something out."

"What's that?"

"Are you a good guy or a bad guy?"

"Neither. I'm just a man trying to hold his own."

"That's not the way it looks."

"Appearance can disguise truth."

"And your truth is?"

A corner of his mouth lifted. "That when I finally fell in love, it was with the wrong woman." He looked at Kyra. "What's your truth? Or are you so used to lying to people who trust you that you've lost yours?"

His words cut like a knife because they were true.

"Go to bed, Kyra."

Kyra straightened away from the railing and walked slowly back to her room. She didn't bother to undress. She didn't even bother to climb beneath the sheets. Instead, she just lay on the bedspread and pulled a corner of it over her.

She was more tired than she'd ever been in her life. She didn't want to think. She didn't want to feel. She just wanted to fall into a deep unconsciousness.

But her mind wouldn't let her.

She had lain there a long time—it seemed like hours—when Kyra heard the soft knock on her door.

She lay still, saying nothing.

She heard the door open. Though she didn't open her eyes, she knew it was Jack.

He stood in the doorway, looking into her room. Entering, he closed the door and stood beside the bed looking down at her.

Kyra started to hold her breath, then realized what

she was doing and continued to breathe normally, rhythmically.

What was he doing? she wondered.

He just stood there, staring at her. She sensed him leaning over her. It was all she could do to keep her body from tensing.

She felt Jack's warm hand on her forehead, pushing her hair away from her face. It was a gentle touch, tender. She wanted to open her eyes and look into his.

What was he thinking?

What was he feeling?

Oh, Jack, she thought with an inward cry.

She heard him cross the room and waited for the door to close.

It didn't.

He was still there. Kyra could feel him in the room with her.

And then she heard him sit in a chair. He let out a long, tired sigh.

After a few minutes, Kyra dared to open her eyes just the narrowest of slits. There was very little light in the room. Just what came in from the moon and stars through the airy drapes.

Jack had leaned his head against the back of the chair, his legs stretched out in front of him. He was still watching her, but she knew that he couldn't tell that she was watching him as well.

He didn't move.

Her eyes gradually fluttered closed and Kyra fell into a genuine sleep.

Jack didn't. He sat there all night, wondering what to do about Kyra.

It wasn't until the first glimmering of daylight that he left her room and entered the main suite. Barry was just getting off the elevator, looking somewhat the worse for wear.

"What are you doing up so early?" he asked, then smirked as he glanced at Kyra's door. "Or need I ask?"

Jack looked at Barry disdainfully. "Grow up, Barry. Get some control over your mouth. And your life."

"Touchy, touchy."

"Don't push me, Barry. I've had it up to the eyebrows with you and your antics. Your amusement value is wearing very thin."

Barry raised a hand in surrender. "Okay. Sorry."

Jack walked into his room and closed the door firmly behind him.

Barry went to the bar and dropped all pretense of casualness when he poured himself a drink with a shaking hand and downed it in one long swallow.

He had problems. Big problems. And if he didn't get them straightened out in the next twenty-four hours, heaven help him.

In her private suite, Kyra woke…alone. She lay in bed, watching the play of the morning sunlight on the walls of her room.

She knew she'd slept, but she was still exhausted. And as sad as she'd ever been.

She remembered Jack in her room the night before.

Her eyes went to the chair, empty now.

She opened her bedroom door and looked into the main suite. It was deserted. She'd half expected Jack to have guards posted, but he'd apparently decided to trust her. At least about this.

Closing the door to her room, she showered, dressed and packed. Unwilling to face Jack just yet, she stepped onto the veranda. It was still early. The beach was bathed in a wonderful, rich, golden light.

Sitting in one of the chairs, she propped her feet up on the railing and breathed deeply of the salty air.

It really was wonderful here. And it was deserted this morning, except for a lone runner in the distance.

As the runner came closer, she realized it was Jack.

The man was a work of art, and her body had the same reaction to him that it would probably always have—a slow melting of her insides.

Every muscle on his dark torso and long, strong legs strained with effort. His face was a picture of pain as his bare feet hammered the surf-wet sand.

When he was nearly in front of the hotel, Jack splashed into the water and dove into the surf. In a few moments he surfaced and with strong, rhythmic strokes, swam farther and farther away from land until he was a mere speck on the horizon.

Kyra rose from her chair and squinted her contact-lensed eyes to track him. After a time, she could tell he was returning to shore. She reclaimed her seat, propped her feet up on the railing and watched as Jack swam closer to land, finally rising like a god from the surf, water running in a sheet down his body.

He spotted Kyra as he walked toward the hotel and changed direction, crossing the sand until he stood in front of her.

She hadn't counted on that. Act normally, she counseled herself. Just act normally. Raising her hand, she shaded her eyes from the sun so she could see him better. "That was a punishing workout," she said.

Jack studied her for a long moment. "Did you sleep well?" he asked, ignoring her remark.

Kyra lowered her feet. "I think so. How about you?"

"I haven't been to bed yet."

"That's two nights with almost no sleep. You must be exhausted."

He didn't say anything.

Kyra cleared her throat. "I'm packed. Where exactly are we going?"

"Home," he said.

"Will I be able to see Noah and my aunt?"

"Of course. I didn't kidnap them, Kyra. I only sent them to a safe place."

She nodded.

"We'll leave in about twenty minutes."

She watched as he walked away from her, struggling not to think of him as a man, but as the subject of an investigation.

And once this was over, she wouldn't think of him at all.

Even as she had the thought, Kyra shook her head. She knew that there wouldn't be a day that went by for the rest of her life when she wouldn't think of Jack Allessandro.

She stayed where she was long after Jack had gone, staring at the water. She was absolutely amazed at how calm she felt. She knew it wouldn't last, of course. Riley would either move in now or take the investigation to the next level. She really didn't know.

As far as what was going to happen to Jack, she had no control over that.

The nearby screech of a seagull knocked her out of her reverie. She looked at her watch. Time to go.

Rising from her chair, she collected her suitcase and carried it into the main suite. Jack came out of his room at the same time.

"Barry," he called out. "Let's go."

Barry came out of his room, dark circles under his eyes, his face haggard and unshaven. She'd never seen him look so unkempt.

"Are you all right?" Kyra asked in concern as she walked toward him.

"Not really, no," he answered. "I feel like hell, actually."

"The sooner we get on the jet, the sooner you can rest up at home," Jack said.

"I'm not going back with you today. I'm far too sick. I think I'll just stay here a day or two until I'm better and then take public transport back to Chicago."

"Are you sure that's what you want to do?" Jack asked pointedly.

"Yeah. There's no sense in my passing on to the two of you whatever bug it is I have. All that time on a jet, breathing the same air, you won't be able to avoid it."

Kyra touched his forehead with the back of her hand. He was perfectly cool to the touch, and yet he was perspiring profusely. It looked like a bad case of nerves to her, but she kept her thoughts to herself.

"Forget it, Barry. You're going with us," Jack said.

"I'm not even packed."

"Leave your things here."

Kyra sympathetically patted Barry on the shoulder, then picked up her own things and followed Jack onto the elevator and out to the helicopter.

With his hands at her waist, Jack helped her on board. Kyra closed her eyes, fighting against the sensation that raced through her body every time the man touched her.

It was over as soon as he released her.

Kyra sat down and buckled herself in. Jack sat beside her and Barry across from her.

"We'll be taking off in a few minutes," said the pilot, talking over his shoulder.

Kyra turned her head to look at Jack and tried to imagine what she would be saying to him if things were normal; if she hadn't overheard what he'd said yesterday; if she were in fact his assistant and had made love with him such a short time before.

Her gaze moved over his profile.

He turned his head to look at her. "What?" he asked in a low voice.

"I was just thinking that if ever there was a man I could have fallen in love with, it was you."

"You're kidding yourself, Kyra. You *are* in love with me. And no matter what you think I am or what you believe I've done, that's not going to change."

The helicopter took off. There was no more chance for conversation, which was fine with Kyra. She had nothing to say.

She knew Jack was right.

She was silent for the rest of the flight and stayed that way as they boarded the jet.

Barry boarded first, grabbed a pillow and blanket and curled up in one of the chairs. Kyra took one of the recliners and Jack sat across from her. He opened a newspaper and began to read. "Damn," he said suddenly as he tossed the newspaper aside. "I left my briefcase in the helicopter. I'll be right back."

Kyra leaned forward and went through different sections of the newspaper until she found one she was interested in.

The copilot walked past her and smiled as he went to the small kitchen and got himself some water. "We should be taking off in a matter of minutes. Mr. Allessandro will be in front with us for a time."

"How long will the flight be?"

"Eight hours, give or take. Better buckle up."

She did. The man sealed the jet and minutes later they were waiting in line with the other jets for take-off.

It wasn't until they'd been in the air for an hour that Kyra unbuckled herself and wandered around the jet. Tired as she was, she couldn't relax.

Something was niggling at her. It was just a feeling.

Walking to the front of the jet, she tapped on the cockpit door and opened it, fully expecting not to find Jack there.

Chapter 14

Jack turned in his seat. "What do you want?" he asked.

Kyra couldn't bring herself to say she was checking on him. "Sorry to bother you, but my watch has stopped. Would you tell me the time?"

"In Chicago?" asked the copilot.

"Yes."

The man told her and she left, closing the door behind her and returning to her seat.

So Jack had reboarded, after all. Would wonders never cease?

After another hour, Jack came into the main cabin. Without saying anything, he took off the black sport coat he was wearing and tossed it over the back of a chair, then stretched out on the couch and lay down, his arm behind his head, eyes closed.

Kyra's eyes moved over his tight jeans inch by

inch, coming to rest on the bulge that left little to the imagination.

Her body responded with a surge of desire that she had no control over. Her mind might have decided that she wasn't going to sleep with him again, but her body wasn't listening.

How was it possible, she wondered, to force herself not to be attracted to Jack? Especially when she had the memory of just how right the two of them were together; how perfectly his body fit hers.

He filled her physically and emotionally to the point where her body literally yearned for his touch, his caress.

No matter what happened from this point forward, Kyra knew she was looking at the only man who would ever make her feel this way.

Part of her loved him for showing her how it could be.

And part of her hated him for damning her to live the rest of her life without ever feeling it again.

She watched him a few minutes longer, then left her chair to take a blanket from the closet. As she walked to where he lay, she pulled down the window shades except for the one by the table, blocking out most of the light.

After shaking the folds out of the blanket, she leaned over Jack and spread the blanket over him.

His hand suddenly shot out from behind his head and grabbed her wrist. Their faces were only inches apart.

Kyra's heart flew into her throat as she looked into his eyes. All she had to do was move forward, just a little, and their lips would touch. She could be in his arms one more time.

She knew Jack wanted her.

She also knew that he wouldn't do anything unless she made the first move.

It was her hesitation that saved her. Jack slowly released her wrist and closed his eyes. "Thank you." His voice was deep and scratchy from fatigue.

Kyra went back to the table and sat with her chin in her hands, and stayed that way until the jet landed in Chicago.

Jack awoke the moment the jet touched down. By the time it came to a full stop, he'd thrown water on his face, tucked in his shirt and put on his jacket.

It took only minutes for them to clear Customs because they had so little luggage, then Jack walked Kyra to a car in front of the airport and put her into the rear seat. "The driver will take you to your family."

"Where are you going?"

"Barry and I have some unfinished business to take care of."

"Jack...?"

He leaned in through the open window and cupped her cheek in his hand. His thumb lightly stroked her soft skin as he looked into her eyes. "Goodbye, Kyra."

As the car pulled away, Kyra realized that his "goodbye" was final. He didn't intend to see her again.

She turned in her seat to look through the rear window.

Jack was still there. And he stayed there until the car was out of sight.

She wanted to stop the car so she could run back to him.

And she wanted to get away as far and as fast as she could.

Every emotion she had about the man was a contradiction.

In the end, she forced herself to sit still for the forty-five minutes it took the car to arrive in downtown Chicago in front of the Palmer House. The driver opened the door for her and handed her a key card. "They're in room 425."

"Thank you," Kyra said, taking the card.

She walked quickly through the lobby to an open elevator and pressed four. Moments later, she was on the fourth floor. Noah and Emily's room was a right turn and ten doors down the hall.

Opening the door of the suite with the card, she fully expected Noah to come running at her, but the sitting room was empty.

"Hello?" she called as she moved farther into the suite. "Noah? Emily?"

Riley appeared in the doorway of the bedroom. "They're at the pool," he said.

"Riley!" she said in surprise. "What are you doing here? How did you know Emily and Noah were here?"

"I got a call from someone who got a call from someone who got a call. You know, the usual."

"Who started the chain of calls?"

"Your friend Allessandro."

"Jack?"

"That's right."

"I'm not following you. Why would he...?"

Riley waved her onto the couch. "Have a seat, Kyra. It's a long story."

Kyra took a chair instead and curled her feet beneath her. "Okay. I'm listening."

"I want to start by telling you that your initial instincts were right. Jack Allessandro hasn't now nor has he ever smuggled any American secrets to anyone."

Relief flooded through her. But there was a slight reality check. "What about the meeting in the warehouse?"

"Set up by the FBI."

"What?" Kyra was as shocked as she sounded. "And they didn't tell us?"

"You know, competition. Apparently your Jack keeps closer track of his business dealings than most men in his position. He noticed a pattern in the purchase of scrap from certain dealers and the sale and shipment to China and Iran. He ran it by a friend of his in the FBI. The FBI was already leagues ahead of us in their investigation when we started. Their investigation led them to Burton Banacomp and Jack's partner, not to mention the Spanish connection."

"So Jack knew?"

"That's right. And it's a good thing he figured it out, because we would have caught on eventually on our own and Jack Allessandro would have been toast. Over the months that Barry has been operating, he's made sure that every piece of paper, every phone call, every computer entry, points directly to Jack. If Allessandro hadn't contacted the FBI, we would have had no reason to look at Barry. Jack would be taking the fall even as we speak.''

"Of course," she said. "That's why Barry wanted to use Jack's computer and phone when Jack was out of the office. What about the cousin?''

"He was involved in a peripheral way, more to get back at Jack than to make a profit. He's been picked up, nonetheless.''

"And Franco Zamora?''

"In custody, along with the dock supervisor and Burton Banacomp and the people who knowingly sold that scrap.''

"When did all this take place?''

"While you were en route to Chicago.''

"And Jack knew it?''

"That's right. He apparently got a little nervous about your family, afraid that Zamora would figure out your involvement and try to use your family as leverage.''

"He told me he'd put them in a safe place.''

"And you believed him? Even after what you'd heard on the docks?''

"Completely.''

Riley shook his head. "I'll never understand women. Not if I live to be a hundred.''

"Which we all hope you do. It's not that complicated, you know. Even if Jack was doing something illegal, I knew he'd never do anything to hurt Noah or me.''

"But *how* did you know that?''

Kyra shrugged. "I just did.''

"See what I mean? Women.''

"Where's Jack now?''

"On his way to Washington. He has meetings and depositions to give."

"What will happen to Barry and Carl?"

"I think Barry's going to get the book thrown at him. Carl, on the other hand—who knows? I guess it depends on how much he knows and how much he's willing to help them make their case."

Kyra let out a long sigh.

"Tired?"

"You have no idea."

Riley smiled. "Anxious to start that desk job, eh?"

"After I take a little time off." She looked at her boss. "Do you think I'll have to testify in this case?"

"I doubt it. Nothing you uncovered was new. You overheard the meeting in the warehouse, but the FBI had it bugged."

"Good. I just want to put this whole experience behind me."

"What about Allessandro?"

Kyra dragged her fingers through her hair. "I have to talk to him."

"Do you think talking will help?"

"I don't know," she said softly. "I just don't know."

"You're in love with him, aren't you?"

A corner of her mouth lifted. "Is it that obvious?"

"I'm afraid so, dear. Even to my old and increasingly cloudy eyes. Are the feelings reciprocated?"

"I don't know. They may once have been."

"But not now?"

"I've lied to him."

There was a small commotion outside the door and then Noah burst into the room, wrapped in a towel, his hair wet. His face lit up at the sight of his mother. Kyra kneeled on the floor and opened her arms. ''Noah!''

Boxes were everywhere. Kyra was leaning over one of them, carefully placing a wrapped stack of dishes.

''Why don't you try calling Jack again?'' her aunt encouraged as she worked beside her.

''I've left five messages in the past two days. If he wanted to talk to me, he would have called.''

''Perhaps he's still out of town.''

''He might be, but I'm sure he's picked up his messages. He doesn't want to speak with me.''

''So you're just going to give up?''

''No. I know we have to talk. I just have to wait until he's ready.'' Kyra sat back on her heels. ''You didn't see the way he looked at me the last time we saw each other.''

Her aunt touched Kyra's hair. ''I'm so sorry.''

''I love him,'' she said softly. ''I don't know what I'm going to do if I have to spend the rest of my life without him.''

''You'll survive. It won't be easy, but you will.''

As Kyra looked at her aunt, her gaze softened. ''Just like you did when your husband died.''

''He was the love of my life. And when I lost him, I lost a part of myself. Not a day goes by that I don't think of him, that I don't miss him. But life goes on and we who are left behind have to move forward.''

''You're a very strong woman,'' Kyra said.

''So are you, dear. Whatever the outcome, you'll be able to handle it.''

Kyra embraced her aunt. "I love you."

Emily's eyes welled with tears. "I love you, too."

It was after business hours but not too late when Kyra arrived at the office. As she'd expected, no one was there. She put a box on top of her desk and began to clear out her drawers, putting her personal things in it.

There wasn't much.

She had just about finished when Jack suddenly walked in.

He stopped dead in the doorway and looked at her. "What are you doing here?"

Kyra touched the box and tried to sound more calm than she felt. "Just getting my things."

"Are you going back to Virginia?"

She nodded. "That's where my home is."

"So that much was true."

"A lot of what I told you was true."

"And a lot wasn't."

"We need to talk," said Kyra.

"Why? So you can clear your conscience?"

"Because there are things you need to hear. Things I couldn't say before."

Jack looked at her for a long moment. "Why not? It might prove enlightening."

He walked into his office and Kyra followed him.

"Which lie do you want to start with?" he asked as he took off his jacket and tossed it on the couch, then loosened his tie as he sat in his chair.

Kyra didn't sit. "First of all, I came here to do a job. An important one. You were suspected of compromising our national security and I was sent here to find information that would indicate if that was true or not.''

Jack didn't say anything.

''I've infiltrated corporations half a dozen times before in my career. This was supposed to be business as usual.''

''Is that what it was when we made love? Business as usual?''

''That's never happened before. And it had nothing to do with business. I fell in love with you before I even realized what had happened. I couldn't stop what was happening between us that night any more than you could.''

Jack was suddenly on his feet, clearly agitated, as he walked to the window.

''You don't know how hard I tried to find evidence that you were innocent. And when I overheard that conversation at the warehouse—''

''You were ready to believe the worst of me, this man you supposedly loved.''

''What else could I think?''

Jack turned to look at her, his eyes blazing. ''You betrayed me over and over again, with every lie, every look, every kiss.'' He shook his head. ''For the first time in my life, I fell in love—with you. I couldn't look at another woman much less touch one. You were the one I'd been waiting for all those years, the one I wanted to have my children, the one I wanted to wake up beside every morning for the rest of my life, the one I wanted to hold in my arms as we fell asleep every night. It turns out that I don't even know who you are.''

''I'm the woman you fell in love with,'' Kyra said.

"You're an investigator with the Department of Justice and, as it turns out, a very good liar. The woman I thought I knew—the one I thought I fell in love with—never existed. She was a figment of your imagination—and mine, as it turned out."

"Give me a chance, Jack. Get to know me now when there are no more secrets between us, no more lies."

Jack walked toward Kyra, stopping in front of her. With his finger under her chin, he raised her face and gazed into her eyes.

Time seemed to stop.

"No," he said. "I will never again allow myself to be that vulnerable to any woman. Particularly you."

A warm tear dropped onto Kyra's cheek and rolled over his finger. "But you loved me."

Jack swallowed hard. "I still love you. But I'll get over it." His hand dropped to his side. "Goodbye, Kyra."

There was nothing more she could say.

Jack walked away from her, back to the window, and stared outside. As far as he was concerned, she was already gone.

Kyra watched him for a moment longer, then straightening her shoulders, she turned to leave, closing the door behind her.

Picking up her box, she took the elevator to the garage, unlocked her car and put the box inside the liftgate.

It wasn't until she was inside the car that she let the sobs she'd been holding back wrack her body.

Chapter 15

It was the middle of the night when the phone rang. Kyra reached for it in the dark and put it to her ear. "Hello?"

"Kyra?"

She recognized the voice and was instantly alert. "Patty?"

"I'm sorry to bother you at this hour."

Kyra sat up. "Is everything all right? Is Jack—?"

"Jack's fine. It's Grandmother. She's in the hospital and failing fast. She wanted me to call you to ask if you'd come to see her before she dies. I wouldn't be doing this if it hadn't seemed so important to her."

"I'll catch the next flight out."

"Thank you, Kyra. I knew I could count on you. I'll tell her to expect you."

Just as Kyra hung up, her aunt walked in, wrapping herself in her robe. "Is everything all right?"

"I have to go to Chicago. Jack's grandmother is dying and wants to see me."

"Make the arrangements and get yourself ready. I'll throw some things into a suitcase for you."

"Thanks, Aunt Emily."

Kyra called the airline and booked herself on a flight. Less than an hour and a half later, she was on her way to Chicago.

It was the wee hours of the morning when she landed and had the taxi take her straight to the hospital.

Patty heard Kyra's footsteps and looked up from where she sat. "Kyra!" she said as she rose and walked toward her. "Thank you so much for coming."

"How's your grandmother?"

"Not well. It's her heart."

"Did she have an attack?"

"Nothing that dramatic. It's just worn-out," said Patty sadly.

Kyra put her arm around Patty's shoulders. "I'm so sorry. What can I do?"

"You're here. That's enough for now. Grandmother's been asking for you ever since she was brought in."

"Do you know why?"

"She won't tell me. She just asked me to call you. She wants to see Jack, too. He's on his way back from the hearings in Washington." She looked down the empty corridor. "I'll tell her you're here."

Kyra waited while Patty went into the room. She came out a moment later and signaled to Kyra.

Kyra took a deep breath and walked the few short

yards to the open door of the dimly lit private room. The older woman lay on the bed, her tiny form barely a bump beneath the white sheet and blanket. Machines were everywhere.

She looked at Kyra and smiled. "Hello, dear."

Patty backed out of the room and closed the door as Kyra moved to a chair beside the bed. "Hello, Mrs. Allessandro."

"Thank you for coming. I have something to talk to you about. It's been nagging at me and won't let me rest."

"What?"

"You and my grandson."

Kyra lowered her eyes.

"Don't look away, child. You love him. I know you do. I've known it since the first time I saw you look at him."

"How I feel about Jack doesn't matter. I betrayed his trust. He'll never forgive me for that."

"He will in time."

"You didn't see the expression on his face when he sent me out of his life. He meant it. There's no room in his heart for forgiveness."

"Kyra, my grandson has waited all his life for the woman meant to be his. You're the one. There will never be another for him. Nothing you've done can change that."

Kyra's throat closed with emotion.

"He needs time to heal. Don't just walk away from him."

"I didn't walk away. Jack sent me."

The door behind her opened. Kyra turned her head to find Jack standing there. Even now, in her eyes, he was the most magnificent of men. Every time she saw him, her heart leaped.

"What are you doing here?" he asked Kyra as he walked farther into the room to stand across from her on the other side of his grandmother's bed.

"I invited her," said the older woman.

"Why?"

"So I could talk to the two of you about what you're doing."

Jack gently took her frail hand in his. "You shouldn't be worrying about us. You need to concentrate on getting better."

"I'm not going to get better," she said matter-of-factly. "You know it and I know it. And I don't want to leave this earth without knowing that you and Kyra are together."

Jack met Kyra's eyes. "There are problems," he said tersely.

"But none that can't be overcome."

Jack was silent.

His grandmother squeezed his hand. "Have you thought about the fact that if you push Kyra far enough away, you could lose her forever? Can you contemplate spending the rest of your life without her?

"And you," she continued as she looked at Kyra "are you going to stand by and let Jack throw away what I know is between you? Will there ever be a man you love as much as you love Jack?"

"I know there won't be," Kyra said.

"And will there ever be a woman you love as much as you love Kyra?"

"No," he said quietly.

"Then get past all of this nonsense and come together. For me, if not for yourselves. I won't be able to rest until I know things are all right between you."

Jack softened. "Grandmother—"

"I've never asked you for anything before, Jack." She paused for a moment and closed her eyes as if she was too exhausted to finish. "I want the two of you to get married right here and now."

"That's not possible. There are forms that have to be filled out, tests that need to be taken."

"You have the power, Jack. You can make it happen. Please."

"Grandmother, we give you our word that we'll try to work things out."

She shook her head. "No. I know you both too well. You'll make a halfhearted effort because you promised me you would, and then you'll separate. If you're married, you'll have no choice but to work things out. The two of you are meant to be together." She grew agitated and one of her monitors began beeping. A nurse came in and quickly adjusted the old woman's oxygen.

"Please," said the nurse, "she needs to stay calm. If you're going to upset her, you'll have to leave."

Jack looked helplessly at Kyra.

"I'll do it if you will," Kyra said.

"I'll make some calls," he said aloud as he leaned toward his grandmother and kissed her forehead. "Everything's going to be fine. Just rest for now."

He took Kyra's arm and steered her from the room. "Thank you," he said. "You fill in Patty while I make the arrangements."

"Fill in Patty about what?" asked his sister.

"Your grandmother wants Jack and me to get married. Does she know about me and what I did?"

"Yes, we all do."

"And it doesn't matter?"

"It hurt Jack, so of course it matters. But it hurts him more to be without you. And you love him. So when is the wedding?"

"Now. This minute."

Patty's eyes widened. "Why, that little stinker. I take it the two of you agreed?"

"We really didn't have a choice. But it'll be in name only. As soon as is practical, we'll dissolve the marriage."

"Is that what Jack said?"

"We haven't had time to discuss it, but I'm sure that's his intention. It's the only reasonable solution."

Jack returned a few minutes later. "I've got the priest on his way over here. The paperwork is being done as we speak." He looked at Kyra. "Can you be ready in an hour?"

"Ready? What do I need to do?"

"Wear a dress, for one," said Patty, eyeing Kyra's trousers and taking her by the elbow. "We'll find something ravishing. Jack, go downstairs and get her some flowers from the gift shop. White, I think, with maybe a little pink."

Patty took Kyra straight to Neiman Marcus and pulled dress after dress off the racks until she found just the right one while a bewildered Kyra stood silently by. It was a white square-neck dress with long sleeves, fitted at the waist with a wide belt and a skirt that flared out. They quickly found matching shoes, and to Kyra's amazement, the perfect hat. When Kyra was completely dressed, Patty stood back and beamed. "You look like a blond Audrey Hepburn," she pronounced. "Perfect for a hospital wedding."

The saleswoman packed Kyra's casual clothes into a bag and handed it to Patty.

The two of them walked outside and straight into a taxi that took them back to the hospital.

Jack had changed into a dark suit. He was standing in the hallway when Kyra got off the elevator. His gaze locked on to hers the moment he saw her and didn't waver until she was by his side. "You look beautiful," he said.

His words, or perhaps it was the tone of his voice, thrilled her. "I hope your grandmother thinks so."

"She will. Are you ready?"

Kyra took a deep breath. "As ready as I'll ever be."

Taking Kyra's arm, Jack led her into the hospital room.

At the sight of the two of them, the old woman's eyes lit up with pleasure. "You both look wonderful." She turned her head toward the priest. "Aren't they the most handsome-looking couple you've ever seen?"

The priest smiled. "They are indeed a good pair."

Jack went to the bedside table and picked up a bouquet of white and pink flowers that he handed to Kyra.

Kevin had arrived and winked at Kyra as he stood beside his wife.

"Are we all here?" asked the priest.

"Yes," said Jack.

"Then we'll get started."

He began with a small talk about what marriage meant and how it shouldn't be entered into lightly. Kyra was numb. She couldn't believe this was happening.

And then she heard Jack's voice vowing to love her forever, and her own voice vowing to love him forever.

The priest asked Jack to place a ring on Kyra's finger.

Jack's grandmother opened her hand to reveal a beautiful antique diamond ring. "This," she said in a weak voice, "is my gift to you. It was given to me by a man I loved from the moment I saw him, just as you two have loved each other in that way. I hope it will bring you both the same happiness and contentment it brought us for more than fifty years."

Jack took it from her palm and kissed her cheek. "Thank you, Grandmother," he said softly. Then he turned to Kyra and took her trembling hand in his. He looked straight into her eyes as he slid it onto her finger and said the words that bound them together.

"I now pronounce you husband and wife," said the priest. "You may kiss the bride."

Kyra wasn't aware that she was crying. Jack reached up to cup her face in his hands. He kissed the warm saltiness on first one cheek and then the other, and then tenderly kissed her lips.

Patty and Kevin both clapped.

Kyra went to the old woman's bedside, leaned over and kissed her cheek. "The ring is beautiful. Thank you."

A nurse, who had been standing off to one side, stepped up to take Mrs. Allessandro's pulse. "I think she's had enough excitement for now,'' she said quietly. ''Let her rest.''

The old woman's eyes still sparkled. ''I'll have an eternity to rest. Let me enjoy the moment.''

Jack took her hand in his. ''The nurse is right. We'll come back later.''

When they were all in the hallway, Kyra touched Jack's arm. ''Don't worry about the ring. I'll return it.''

Jack put his hand over hers. ''My grandmother gave it to you.''

''She gave it to us. There is no us. I just want you to know that before I leave Chicago, I'll get the ring to you. It should be on the finger of the woman you love.''

Jack started to say something, but stopped when Patty approached. ''We should celebrate with a champagne brunch,'' she said.

Kyra took off her hat and shook her hair free. ''Not for me, thank you. I just want to go to my hotel and change clothes.''

''Did you bring a suitcase?'' asked Kevin.

''Yes. I left it with the information desk in the lobby.''

''Where will you be staying?'' asked Patty.

''I don't know. I haven't really thought about it. The Palmer House, I suppose.''

''I'll take you,'' said Jack.

''I can catch a taxi.''

He put his arm around her waist. ''After what you just did for my grandmother, it's the least I can do.'' He looked at his sister. ''I'll be back in an hour.''

They were silent on the walk to his car. After opening the door for her, Jack put her suitcase into the trunk, started the engine and pulled into traffic. Neither said anything on the ride to the hotel. Jack checked her in himself and took her in the elevator to her room. Using the key card, he opened the door for her and carried her suitcase inside.

Taking her hand in his, he folded her fingers around the key card. "Thank you for coming."

"I love your grandmother."

"She feels the same way about you. I can't tell you how grateful I am that you helped me put her mind at ease."

Kyra didn't say anything.

"She isn't expected to live much longer," he said, his voice thick with emotion before he cleared his throat. "Maybe a day or two. If you could stay in Chicago until afterward, I'd appreciate it."

"Of course I will."

He let go of her hand. "I'll pick you up in the morning so we can see her together."

"What time?"

"Nine?"

"I'll be ready."

"See you then."

Jack left and closed the door behind him, jiggling the handle to make sure it was locked.

Kyra walked to the dresser and tossed the key card on top. For a long time, she stared at her reflection in the mirror. This was how she looked on her wedding day.

Alone.

She stayed in her room for the rest of the day, pacing and thinking. Toward evening, she ordered room service and turned on the television. It was only ten o'clock when she finally went to bed.

Just like the night before, the ringing of the phone awakened her in the middle of the night. This time, though, she answered it anxiously, knowing it could mean only one thing.

"Kyra, this is Kevin."

She sat up on the edge of the bed. "What's wrong?"

"Grandmother died about an hour ago."

"Oh, Kevin. I'm so sorry."

"She was ready to go. Both Patty and Jack were with her."

"Is there anything I can do?"

"Yes, actually. And I apologize for asking this, but Patty and I don't know what else to do."

"Go ahead."

"Jack left the hospital a little while ago. He doesn't want to admit it, but I know he's very upset. I think his grandmother is one of the few people in his life that Jack genuinely loved. He won't talk to Patty or me, but he might talk to you."

"I really doubt that."

"He needs you, Kyra."

It took her a moment to answer. "All right. I'll go."

"Thanks. It'll be a big relief to Patty. We told building security to expect you."

As soon as she hung up, Kyra pulled on a pair of jeans and a T-shirt, brushed her hair but didn't bother with makeup.

The lobby of the hotel was deserted and there was

a lone cab on duty in front. She jumped in and gave him the address.

Chicago was beautiful at night. No pedestrians. It must have rained earlier in the evening because the pavement was wet and reflected the amber glow of the streetlights. The driver didn't talk and wasn't playing the radio, so it was just the sound of the car and the swoosh of the tires on the wet asphalt.

The cab stopped in front of Jack's building. Kyra quickly paid him and walked into the lobby through the revolving glass doors. She was surprised to see the same man who was usually on duty during the day. She didn't know his name, but he knew who she was. "Ms. Courtland, how are you? Mr. Allessandro's sister called and said I should let you go straight up to the apartment. Would you like me to call him first?"

"No." She knew that Jack would probably tell him to send her away.

"All right. Please give him my condolences on the loss of his grandmother. I met her a few times. She was a fine woman."

"Yes, she was. And I will. Thank you."

He followed her to the elevator and inserted the card that would allow her to travel to the penthouse, then stepped off and watched as the doors closed between them.

The elevator only took a few seconds to travel to the top of the building. The doors opened into a darkened foyer. Kyra stepped out, but stayed where she was for a few moments while her eyes adjusted to the darkness. "Hello?" she called softly. "Are you here, Jack? It's me, Kyra."

There was no answer.

She walked farther into the apartment, and was finally able to see a little better because of the moonlight coming in through the windows.

There was Jack, in the living room, standing in front of a huge window, staring outside.

"Jack?"

He didn't turn around. "What are you doing here?"

"Kevin called. He told me about your grandmother. I'm so sorry."

He didn't say anything.

"Are you all right?" she asked as she moved closer to him.

"I'll be fine. Right now I just want to be left alone."

Reaching out a gentle hand, she rested it on his strong arm. "I know how much you loved her."

He was silent.

"If you want to talk, I'm here to listen."

He continued to stare out the window. Kyra saw a tear roll down his cheek. She would have been willing to bet that was the first tear he'd shed since childhood.

She moved in front of him and raised her hand to his cheek.

Jack grabbed her wrist and jerked her hand away from his face. "Don't touch me."

"Why?"

He glared at her.

"Why?" she asked again. "Are you ashamed of what you're feeling?" She raised her other hand to his face. "Are you ashamed to let me see your tears?"

This time Jack put his hand gently over hers and closed his eyes. Kyra stepped closer. She couldn't bear to see him in such pain. Raising up on her toes, she kissed the corner of his eye, tasting the salty dampness. Then she kissed his cheek.

Jack let out a groan and suddenly locked her in his arms. His mouth came down on hers in a hard kiss that was full of an explosion of suddenly released emotions.

Kyra wrapped her arms around his neck and held on.

He suddenly stopped and pushed her away. "You should leave."

"I'm not going anywhere."

"Kyra, I'm not myself tonight."

"I know. You're open to me for the first time since that night in Spain. Don't close yourself off again. Not now."

"I don't want to hurt you."

"You let me worry about myself. I'm a big girl."

He pulled her into his arms and held her so tightly she thought she would break. She could feel his body shake with each sob, but he was silent.

Kyra pulled her head back and kissed him over and over again.

Jack held her by the shoulders and looked into her eyes. With unexpected and unutterable tenderness, he kissed her long and slow.

Then, still kissing her, he lifted her in his arms and carried her to the bedroom.

As Kyra lay back against the pillows, Jack stood over her, looking down. Her blond hair was spread out, framing her lovely face. Her cheeks were flushed.

Her eyes were filled with the love he knew she felt for him.

He pushed her hair away from her face with a gentle hand, then lowered himself beside her. Pulling her into his arms, he moved slowly, kissing her lingeringly, exploring her with his mouth and hands.

And then Kyra went on a journey of her own, kissing her way down his body, using her mouth and tongue to make his body tense and spasm with pleasure.

When he could stand it no longer, Jack would roll Kyra onto her back and do the same to her.

They made love for hours, bringing each other to the brink and then stopping and just holding each other before starting all over again.

When they finally climaxed, it was together, and with an intensity that made them both cry out.

Jack rolled onto his back, bringing Kyra with him, holding her tightly in his arms as though he never wanted to let her go. He fell asleep that way.

Kyra couldn't sleep. She didn't want to. She just wanted to feel his body beside hers, listen to his deep breaths, smell his clean skin.

It would be the last time.

As the sun began to rise, so did Kyra. She gathered up her clothes, then turned to look at Jack one last time. "I love you," she whispered.

In the living room, she quickly dressed. Going to his desk, she took out paper and pen and wrote him a note.

Please, don't feel any guilt over last night. I knew exactly what I was doing and wouldn't change a second of it. I love you, I always will. More than anything, I wish you could forgive me for my betrayal, but I know that's not to be. By the time you read this, I'll be on my way back to Virginia. As for your grandmother's funeral, I'll be there in spirit if not in body. She knew how I felt about her. Please give my warmest regards to Patty and Kevin.

My love to you, Jack.

Folding the note, she took his grandmother's ring from her finger and placed it gently on top.

Then she left.

Kyra had had to work late. It was dark as she drove down the long driveway of her little farmhouse. There was a car sitting in front that she didn't recognize and Kyra smiled. Her aunt had been growing increasingly social since Chicago and probably had a friend over for cards or something.

Pulling her briefcase off the passenger seat, Kyra walked up the porch steps and in through the unlocked front door.

"Aunt Emily?" she called quietly as she dropped her keys on the hall table and set down her briefcase.

Walking into the living room, she found Jack lying on the couch with a sound-asleep Noah lying on top of him.

When Jack saw her, he raised his finger to his lips to shush her, then sat up while gently picking up Noah in his arms and carrying the little boy to his room.

Kyra followed and watched from the doorway in

amazement as Jack laid Noah down, covered him with a blanket and kissed the side of the child's head.

Walking quietly from the room, he took Kyra's elbow in his hand and turned her around as he closed the door most of the way, then guided her to the living room.

"Your aunt wanted to go to a movie with a friend, so I volunteered to baby-sit."

Kyra couldn't stop looking at him. It seemed like forever since she'd last seen him. "Why are you here?"

"That's exactly what your aunt asked."

"And what did you tell her?"

He looked into her eyes. "That I was a fool to let you go. That I love you more than life itself, and the time I've spent without you has been a living hell."

Kyra couldn't believe what she was hearing.

"I know that legally speaking, we're married. But I never asked you myself. I want to do that now."

He stood in front of Kyra and took her in his arms. "I have never felt anything as powerful as what I feel for you. I felt it the moment you walked into my office. I just didn't know what it was. I wanted to be with you every moment of every day. I wanted you in my bed and in my arms every moment of every night. I wondered where you were and who you were with, and hated the idea of you being with anyone else. You became as much a part of me as the air that I breathe. No one has ever held that kind of power over me. As strongly as I was drawn to you, I pushed myself away—until that night in Spain. Neither of us intended what happened, but it did, and for me it was a defining moment in my life. You were the one. The only one."

Kyra's eyes filled with tears.

"When I found out that you'd been lying to me, it was a harder blow than I'd ever been dealt. I'd never cared before. Now I cared so deeply that I was seared to the core of my being. I withdrew. I grieved for the love I thought I'd lost forever. I convinced myself that I wasn't in love with you because I'd never known the real you."

"What changed?" she asked.

"I did. I realized that the woman I fell in love with was Kyra Courtland, whatever role she was playing at the moment. You weren't putting on an act when you were with your child. You weren't putting on an act when you were with my grandmother. And you certainly weren't putting on an act when we made love. What happened to us was real. My grandmother knew it. That's why she was so anxious to see us married before she died. She knew that if I just gave myself enough time, I'd come to realize what she'd known all along—that we belong together now and forever."

He cupped her face in his hands.

"I guess what I'm saying, Kyra, is that I love you to the depths of my being. I can't imagine a life without you in it—or at least not a life that I'd care to live. I want to stay married to you. I guess the question is, will you stay married to me?"

"I want that more than anything," Kyra whispered in a choked voice.

Jack took his grandmother's ring from his pocket and slid it back onto her finger. Then he raised her hand to his lips and kissed it. "Now it's where it belongs."

Kyra leaned into Jack. He wrapped her tightly in his arms and held her as though he would never let her go. "I love you," she said. "I thought I'd lost you. That I'd never see you again."

"I was a fool, Kyra. But I'll never hurt you like that again. I promise."

Kyra started crying and couldn't stop.

"What's this?" asked Jack as he held her away from him.

"I'm sorry," she said, half crying, half laughing. "I'm so happy it hurts."

Jack pulled her into his arms. He was never going to let her go again.

Epilogue

The Chicago park was teeming with people, some milling around, some in folding chairs, others, like Kyra, sitting on blankets, listening to an Ecuadoran band called *Inkapirka* play their soulful, achingly beautiful South American music.

She was sitting with her legs stretched out in front of her, leaning back on her hands, her face raised toward the sun, eyes closed.

Jack sat beside his wife, his eyes on her enraptured face. "You're so beautiful," he said softly.

Kyra turned her head, her eyes warm with love. "Even though I look more like a beached whale than the woman you married?"

Jack rested his palm lightly on her very pregnant stomach. "You've never been more beautiful than you are at this moment."

Kyra's smile grew. "You really are in love, aren't you?"

He stretched out beside her, raised on one elbow, his head resting on his hand. "More than I ever dreamed possible."

Kyra lay completely back and raised her hand to his face, stroking her fingertips over his darkly shadowed cheeks. "We came so close to not finding our way back to each other."

"I would never have let you go."

"You were very angry with me."

"For good reason. And that anger made me foolish for a time. It almost cost me a life with you. But no matter how angry I was, I never stopped loving you. I never stopped wanting you."

Kyra gave a little gasp and reached for her stomach.

Jack was on instant alert. "What's wrong?"

She took his hand and placed it on the left side of her belly. "Do you feel that?" she asked.

"Something's sticking out."

"It's probably a little foot or elbow."

With his hand still on her, he leaned forward and kissed Kyra gently on the lips. "Before I met you, I think I must have been more dead than alive. I never thought I could feel what you make me feel. And every day it deepens."

Kyra raised her head and lightly brushed her lips against his. "I fell in love with you the moment I saw you. No matter how hard I fought against the feeling, it kept rushing back and overwhelming every logical impulse I had. I can't imagine what the rest of my life would have been like if you hadn't come to your senses." A dimple appeared in her cheek. "Or lost them completely, which is probably more to the point.

And Noah," she said softly, more seriously, "he loves you as though you were his natural father."

"I love him, too."

"He can feel it. That's why he took to you so quickly."

Noah suddenly leaped full force onto Jack's back. "I wanna get popcorn."

Jack smiled at Kyra and kissed her. "Popcorn. Would you like some?"

"A big one."

Jack looked over his shoulder to the older woman standing there. "Is he running you ragged, Emily?"

"Let's just say Noah keeps me in shape." She laughed. "And after dating Riley Hennessey for the past year, I need all of the conditioning I can get."

Riley put his arm around Emily. "Wait until we get married next month."

As he rose, Jack twirled Noah around to sit on his shoulders. "What can I get you, Emily? Riley?"

"I'll come with you," said Riley.

"Surprise me," Emily said.

Jack looked back at Kyra and the expression on his face was one of nearly unfathomable tenderness.

Emily looked from Jack and Noah to her niece. It was as though they had always been a family. And Jack and Kyra had made it clear that they considered her an integral part of their lives. She knew that if she and Riley hadn't found their way to each other, she would have always found a warm and welcoming home with them. As it was, she was still going to be helping with Noah and the new baby.

Jack turned again and looked at them, smiling at Kyra.

Emily touched her niece's hand. .

Kyra looked from Jack and Noah to Riley and then Emily. "I think," she said, "that I'm the luckiest woman in the world."

* * * * *

*If you liked this explosive novel, look for
Brittany Young's next Special Edition,
THE SHEIK'S MISTRESS,
coming in July 1998.
For irresistible heroes, sizzling sexual tension
and classic love stories, Brittany Young
delivers, time after time after time....*

ALL THAT GLITTERS

by *New York Times* bestselling author

LINDA HOWARD

Greek billionaire Nikolas Constantinos was used to getting what he wanted—in business and in his personal life. Until he met Jessica Stanton. Love hadn't been part of his plan. But love was the one thing he couldn't control.

From *New York Times* bestselling author Linda Howard comes a sensual tale of business and pleasure—of a man who wants both and a woman who wants more.

DIANA PALMER
ANN MAJOR
SUSAN MALLERY

RETURN TO WHITEHORN

In **April 1998** get ready to catch the bouquet. Join in the excitement as these bestselling authors lead us down the aisle with three heartwarming tales of love and matrimony in Big Sky country.

A very engaged lady is having second thoughts about her intended; a pregnant librarian is wooed by the town bad boy; a cowgirl meets up with her first love. Which Maverick will be the next one to get hitched?

Available in **April 1998.**

Silhouette's beloved **MONTANA MAVERICKS** returns in Special Edition and Harlequin Historicals starting in February 1998, with brand-new stories from your favorite authors.

Round up these great new stories at your favorite retail outlet.

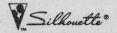